William and the Evacuees

"MR. CHAMB'LAIN SENT ME TO ASK IF YOU C'N
TAKE IN ANY 'VACUEES," SAID WILLIAM.

(see page 11)

William and the Evacuees

RICHMAL CROMPTON

Illustrated by Thomas Henry

MACMILLAN CHILDREN'S BOOKS

First published 1940

Copyright Richmal C. Ashbee

Text illustrations copyright Thomas Henry Fisher Estate

First published in this edition 1987 by
PAN MACMILLAN CHILDREN'S BOOKS
Reprinted 1996 by Macmillan Children's Books
A division of Macmillan Publishers Limited
London and Basingstoke
Associated companies throughout the world

A CIP catalogue record for this book is
available from the British Library

ISBN 0 333 43674 1

7 9 10 8

Phototypeset by Wyvern Typesetting Ltd, Bristol
Printed and bound in Great Britain by
Mackays of Chatham PLC, Chatham, Kent

Contents

William invites you!

Join my club and becum a n Outlaw
William Brown

You can join the Outlaws Club!

You will receive
a special Outlaws wallet containing
your own Outlaws badge
the Club Rules
and
a letter from William giving you
the secret password

To join, send a postal order for £2.50 and a letter
telling us you want to join the Outlaws, with your
name and address written in block capitals, to:

The Outlaws Club
Macmillan Children's Books
25 Eccleston Place
London SW1W 9NF

You must live in the United Kingdom or the
Republic of Ireland in order to join.

Chapter 1

William and the Evacuees

The evacuees' party, given by William and the Outlaws in the studio of Hillside Cottage, had been a great success. Sounds of revelry had, indeed, been heard as far off as the next village, and the guests had departed home in that tattered condition that seemed to be the inevitable result of any game organised by the Outlaws.

It was two days after this that a small deputation of village children waylaid William as he was returning home from the old barn.

"We want to be 'vacuated, too," said Arabella Simpkin, a red-haired long-nosed girl, who automatically constituted herself the leader of any group of which she formed part. "They get all the fun. . . ."

"Yes," grumbled Frankie Miller, a small, stout, snub-nosed boy of seven. "They got a Christmas party *an*' a Christmas tree."

"An' tins of sweets all round," put in Ella Popple-ham, a morose-looking child, with a shock of black hair and a squint. "A whole *tin* of sweets each. It's not fair, it isn't. Puttin' on side an' havin' parties an' eatin' whole *tins* of sweets. It's not fair. We oughter be 'vacuated, too."

"I been 'vacuated," said a small, foursquare child proudly. "It made my arm come up somethin' korful."

"Shut up, Georgie Parker," said Arabella. "It's a diff'rent sort of 'vacuated you have done on your arm. It's to stop you turnin' into a cow you have it done on your arm."

"Thought it was to stop you gettin' chicken pox," said Frankie, wrinkling up his snub nose in perplexity. "Someone *told* me it was to stop you gettin' chicken pox, anyway."

"It's nothin' to do with chickens," snapped Arabella. "It's cows. Everyone what's not 'vacuated on their arms turns into cows. Half the cows you see in fields is people what weren't 'vacuated on their arms."

They stared at her, surprised but impressed. Her tall stature, her long thin nose, her general air of sharpness, gave her words a weight that they would not have had coming from anyone else.

"Well, never mind that," said Maisie Fellowes, a roly poly of a girl, who bore a striking resemblance to Queen Victoria in her old age and who vied with Arabella for leadership of the group. "Never mind that. It's not that sort of 'vacuation, anyway. It's not the sort to do with chickens and cows. It's the sort to do with parties an' tins of sweets. Why, they've all had new scarves an' things knit them while we've gotter wear our old ones what we had all last winter. Well, mine's the one what my sister had. We've had it in the fam'ly for *years*. We never have nothin' new in our fam'ly. Those 'vacuation kids get everythin' new. An' the way they swank makes me sick."

"I was jus' goin' to say all that," put in Arabella, determined not to abandon her position as leader. "An' what I say is, somethin' oughter be *done* about it."

"It swelled up somethin' korful," said Georgie

Parker again, clinging pathetically to his bit of limelight.
"Ever so big. Like a balloon, it was."

"Can't 've been like a balloon," said Ella Poppleham, squinting at him quellingly. "An arm *can't* be like
a balloon."

"Oh, shut up," said Arabella, putting her hands on
her hips and assuming an air of leadership. "You all
keep on talkin' about b'loons an' cows an' chickens
an' things when what we've come to talk about is
'vacuation."

"What I say is," put in Maisie, "we've got to be
'vacuated same as those swanky kids."

"I just said that," snapped Arabella.

"I don't care what you said," countered Maisie,
assuming the expression of Queen Victoria engaged in
putting Mr. Gladstone in his place. "That's what *I* say. I
say we've gotter be 'vacuated. No one gets any fun these
days 'cept 'vacuated kids. Toys an' parties an' tins of
sweets an' everythin' they want."

"It *did* swell up same as a b'loon," put in Georgie
Parker in his deep slow voice. "If you'd seen it you'd 've
said it was same as a b'loon. All red, too, same as a
b'loon. A red b'loon."

"Oh, do shut up about b'loons," said Arabella.

"I don't b'lieve people *do* turn into chickens," said
Carolina Jones, a small child with carefully tended
ringlets and film star eyelashes, who had not spoken yet.
"I've never seen anyone turnin' into a chicken an' I
don't b'lieve anyone does."

"I never said they did turn into chickens," said
Arabella.

"You did."

"I didn't."

"You did."

"I didn't."

"You did."

"I said they turned into cows."

"Well, it's just the same."

"It isn't."

"It is."

"Shut *up*," said Queen Victoria severely. "We're not here to talk about cows an' chickens. We're here to ask William Brown if he can help us get 'vacuated."

William had so far listened in silence. It was not his custom to listen in silence to anything for any length of time, but the situation interested him. He saw the

"I S'POSE THEY DON'T THINK THERE'S MUCH CHANCE OF
YOU GETTIN' BOMBED HERE," SAID WILLIAM.

various points that these would-be evacuees had stressed so strongly, but . . .

"I s'pose they don't think there's much chance of you gettin' bombed here," he said, voicing the obvious objection to the scheme.

They stared at him.

"It's nothin' to do with *bombs*," said Arabella. "Why don't you listen? It's to do with parties an' new clothes an' tins of sweets an' things. Why don't you *listen*?"

"IT'S NOTHIN' TO DO WITH *BOMBS*," SAID ARABELLA.
"WHY DON'T YOU LISTEN?"

"I was listenin'," said William. "I heard everythin' you said."

"Well, they get all the fun an' we don't see why we shun't get a bit, too," said Maisie. "I've never been 'vacuated in all my life," she added pathetically.

"I bet I'd rather 've *been* a cow than had my arm all swelled up like that," put in Georgie. "Like a b'loon, it was. A red b'loon."

"Oh, shut up," said Arabella fiercely. "The way you all go *on*. . . ." She turned to William, her pugnacious expression becoming more formidable than ever as she tried to soften it into one of sweetness, "We thought you'd help to 'vacuate us, William, 'cause you're so clever."

William wasn't proof against this. Quite definitely he did consider himself clever, but very few other people seemed to recognise the fact. Certainly Arabella had never recognised it before. Moreover, he had just been indirectly (as will be recounted hereafter) responsible for bringing to justice a German who was engaged in making plans of aeroplanes at Marleigh Aerodrome. Compared with that, of course, drawing up an evacuation scheme was child's play. In any case, he would not have admitted that he couldn't do it. William never admitted that he couldn't do anything. . . . He assumed his air of omnipotence.

"Well . . ." he said thoughtfully, as if drawing his mind from some weighty problem to deal with a matter of minor importance. "Well . . . I'll have to think about it, of course. I—" yielding suddenly to reason, "I'm not sure I can do it."

"Of course you can, William," said Maisie. "You can do anything, if you want to."

"I know I can," agreed William hastily. "Yes, I know

I can, but I'm not sure that I want to. I mean, I'm busy jus' now. I've got other things to do just now. If you'd come las' week . . ." he went on regretfully. "I wasn't quite so busy las' week. But I'm jolly busy now."

"*Please*, William," said Carolina.

Besides the ringlets and film star eyelashes, she had blue eyes and a cherubic mouth.

William deliberated and was lost. Reason clamoured to be heard, but he turned a deaf ear to it.

"Well, p'raps . . ." he temporised. "I mean, I'm jolly busy just now, but——"

"Oh, *thank* you, William," said Carolina.

"I'm not sure I want to be done again," put in Georgie plaintively. "I bet when you've been done you won't want to be done again, either. It swelled up like a b'loon." .

No one took any notice of him.

"I din't say I'd *do* it," said William hastily. "I said, p'raps. I said I'd think about it."

"But you will do it, won't you?" persisted Arabella. "We thought over everyone we knew, an' we said, 'There's only William Brown could do it.' "

"I said that," put in Maisie. "I said, 'If anyone can, William Brown can.' "

"We said you'd caught that spy las' month," said Arabella, "so if anyone could do it you could."

All this, of course, went to William's head like wine. Reason and discretion vanished in a mist of complacency.

"You *will*, won't you?" said Arabella again.

"All right," said William, with the air of an amused giant granting a pygmy's request. "All right, I will."

"Oh, thank you," said Arabella and Maisie simultaneously.

would," said Ella Poppleham. "I said,
rough boy an' I don't like him, but he *does*
said you'd *do* it."

"A right," said William coldly. "There's lots
rougher than me."

"*I've* not met any," said Ella, who on principle never
neglected the makings of a good quarrel. "You're the
roughest boy I've ever seen, an' the dirtiest."

"Well, *that* doesn't matter," interposed Arabella
generously. "Dirt never stopped anyone *doin'* things."

"I never said it did," snapped Ella.

"You did."

"I didn't."

"You did," said Arabella, fanning the flames.

"Oh, shut up," said Maisie. "How long'll you take,
William?"

"I can't tell," said William, trying to stifle the doubts
that were already rising in his mind. "I can't quite tell
how long it'll take me. You can't with a thing like that."

"But you'll be as quick as you can?" stipulated
Arabella. Now that she had gained her purpose, the
intimidating gleam had returned to her eye, and she was
evidently going to waste no more time on the
uncongenial task of flattery.

"You're so clever, William," said Carolina, shaking
back the ringlets and fluttering the long eyelashes.
"You're so *clever*. Get me somewhere where they'll
give me *lots* of sweets an' some new toys, won't you?"

"I—I'll do my best," said William, secretly aghast at
the thought of the task he had undertaken. "I—I'll
try'n' get you 'vacuated, all right."

"You've got all this afternoon," said Arabella. "You
ought to've fixed somethin' up by to-morrow."

"It's sweet of you, William," said Carolina. "I'd like

a new dolly, an' a new teddy bear. The legs have come off mine."

"I had grapes," said Georgie Parker importantly. "Whole bags of 'em. An' gosh! Din' it swell up . . .!"

William walked homewards slowly and thoughtfully. He didn't actually regret having undertaken the task (he still felt flattered by the confidence reposed in him), but he was beginning to realise its magnitude. To evacuate an indefinite number of children (for he judged rightly that the original number would be considerably increased as the news of the impending evacuation spread), alone and unaided, would, he realised, need all his resources. He felt, however, no desire to retreat from the position he had taken up. Two things alone would have prevented his doing that—the gleam in Arabella's eye (he knew by experience how devastating her scorn and anger could be, and it had been a novel and highly pleasant experience to see her humbly—or almost humbly—mendicant) and the flutter of Carolina's long eyelashes. The flutter expressed an admiration that William would have done much to justify. In fact, he was going to do much. . . . His heart sank again as he considered how much. Then he consoled himself by the reflection that the government had evacuated whole towns in a few hours without a hitch. William considered himself as good as the government any day. . . .

He set out immediately after lunch on a tour of inspection. He must find a place, of course, some distance from his own village. . . . The term evacuation seemed in itself to imply that. . . . A dozen vague—and highly impossible—plans floated through his mind. Could he find some empty house and run the whole thing himself? But even his glorious optimism balked at the prospect. He might find the empty house, he might lead his would-be evacuees to it, but even he realised that he couldn't provide for them once he'd got them there. No, the alternative was—for a moment he couldn't think what the alternative was. . . . Something was certain to turn up, he reassured himself, as he tramped along the road, his brow set and frowning, his face bearing that expression of ferocity that deep thought always imparted to it. He passed through Marleigh and Upper Marleigh. He knew most of the people there. Those who had any superfluous space in their houses had already filled it with official or unofficial evacuees. He knocked at one or two houses and boldly asked if they had any further room for evacuees, but on both occasions he was sent off so unceremoniously that it discouraged him from further efforts.

"You saucy little hound!" said one indignant house-holder.

"You cheeky little rapscallion!" said an enraged housemaid as she slammed the door in his face.

"Bet they never did that to him," he muttered indignantly to himself as he walked on down the road. "Bet they never did that to ole Mr. Chamb'lain when *he* went round gettin' places for 'em. Bet they treated him a bit different. . . ."

He brooded in silence for some moments on a mental picture of Mr. Chamberlain going from door to door and being affably received. . . . He had a wild idea of disguising himself as Mr. Chamberlain, but realised almost at once the futility of the idea. He made one last attempt, and, approaching a smallish house that he thought optimistically might afford shelter to a couple or so of his clients, knocked at the door. A very old woman opened it. She smiled at him pleasantly and said: "Yes dear? What do you want?"

"Mr. Chamb'lain's sent me to ask if you've got any rooms vacant."

"No, dear," she replied. "I didn't order bacon. Just a pound of sausages as usual, and tell him to send before dark."

She was closing the door on him.

"No, wait," he said loudly. "I din' mean that. Listen." He raised his voice still more. "Mr. Chamb'-lain's sent me to ask if you c'n take in any 'vacuees."

She looked at him pityingly.

"What a shame to send a child like you touting for orders!" she said. "No, dear, tell him I've never used a vacuum. I use an old-fashioned broom just as my mother did—with tea leaves if the carpet's very bad. And tell your mother from me that it's a great mistake to let a child of your age take up this sort of work. For one thing it's a blind alley, and for another you're far too young for it." She vanished for a moment, to reappear with a biscuit, which she thrust into his hand. "And now go home and get your tea."

With that she disappeared, leaving him staring at the closed door, the biscuit in his hand. There seemed nothing to do but eat the biscuit, so he proceeded to do that as he walked slowly down to the gate and along the road. . . . After all, even Mr. Chamberlain, he told himself, would have eaten a biscuit if anyone had given him one. But despite the biscuit—and it was a good biscuit—he felt dejected. He'd spent a good deal of time and trouble without any result. He considered the possibility of going back to Arabella and the others and telling them that he hadn't found it possible to arrange for their evacuation. But he shrank from the scorn and anger of the formidable Arabella and from the fading of the light of admiration from Carolina's blue eyes. No, he'd have another shot at fixing something up. . . . A narrow lane ran from the main road. . . . He'd go down that and see if he couldn't find anything. It wouldn't matter if he was a bit late for tea. . . .

He turned into the lane, and was just swallowing the last morsel of his biscuit when he found himself at the gates of a biggish house that bore a vague air of being unoccupied.

Keeping in the shelter of the bushes, he made his way very cautiously up the short drive and peeped in at a large window downstairs. Yes . . . curtains hung at the windows, but the furniture was shrouded in dust sheets. Furnished but unoccupied. . . . Just what he wanted. His spirits rose, and for a moment he felt that he had reached the end of his quest. Then, as gradually the problems still to be overcome presented themselves to him, his spirits sank again. . . . He'd found the place all right, but how was he to settle his evacuees in it? Was the place wholly deserted or might someone be coming back to it any minute? Was anyone left in charge? . . . At that moment an old man wearing a green baize apron entered the room and began to pass a duster in a somewhat half-hearted fashion over the exposed portion of the furniture. Evidently someone *was* in charge. . . . He made a tour round the outside of the house, looking in at all the windows. Everything was deserted, the furniture swathed in dust sheets. A convenient tree assured him that the upper storey was in the same state. He climbed down again and considered the situation. His first instinct was to approach the custodian in the green apron and make immediate arrangements for the reception of his evacuees, but experience had sadly discouraged him. When you did that, people either banged the door in your face or didn't hear what you said. Somehow the old man in the green apron looked as if he might do both. . . . He remembered that on one occasion his mother, wishing to lodge a complaint against some public body, had said, "I shall write about it. They take no notice of you if you just go." William decided to write about it. . . .

He found Arabella and Maisie lying in wait for him on his way home. Arabella's eyes held a gleam that was both propitiatory and intimidating.

"Well," she said, "have you got us fixed up yet?"

"Time you had," said Maisie sternly. "Someone sent down a whole lot of sweets for 'em again this morning."

"Well, yes," said William. "Practically. I mean, I've got you practically fixed up."

"Can we come now, at once?" demanded Arabella.

"Well, not jus' now," said William.

"To-morrow?"

"Well, I think so. I'm not quite sure—not *quite* sure about to-morrow."

"When, then?" said Maisie.

"Well, quite soon now," said William. "I'll let you know as soon as I've got it quite fixed up. I've got it *practically* fixed up, but I'll let you know as soon as I've got it *quite* fixed up."

"When will you let us know?"

"Well . . . I 'spect I can let you know to-morrow."

"But you said we could go to-morrow," objected Arabella, her eyes taking on a Hitlerish gleam. "We've been waitin' hours an' *hours*. You said we could *go* to-morrow."

"Well, p'raps," hedged William. "I meant, p'raps. I mean, I was *practically* sure you could go to-morrow. I bet ole Mr. Chamb'lain di'n't fix it all up in one afternoon. I bet he'd gotter go to ever so many houses first same as what I've had to. I bet I'm doin' it as quick as he did, anyway."

"Well, to-morrow, then," said Arabella. "We'll come round to-morrow an' see if you've got it all fixed up."

"You are *clever*, William," said Carolina.

And that was the sole ray of comfort the situation provided.

Directly after tea William went up to his bedroom to compose the letter. It took much time and trouble. More than once he nearly gave the whole thing up, but again it was the memory of the challenging gleam in Arabella's eye and the admiring gleam in Carolina's that made him decide to go on with it. He tore up several attempts at the letter before he was satisfied, and even then he wasn't *quite* satisfied. . . . "I wish I knew what that ole Chamb'lain man wrote," he muttered as, inkstained, dishevelled and scowling, he examined the final effort.

Dear Sir,
    I am sending you sum evackueys tomorro. Please have everythin ready,

                              Luv from,
                              Mister Chamblane.

Besides the fact that he did not possess the requisite three-halfpence, he was unwilling to commit the precious document to the hazards of the post, so he set off through the gathering dusk to deliver it in person. Again doubts assailed him. Was the place too near home? How would the request be received? Why—oh why—had he ever said he'd do it? And yet again, the very magnitude of the task fascinated him. Other people had organised evacution on a large scale. Surely he could evacuate a mere handful—just a dozen or so. A dozen! Gosh! it was too many. He wished he'd started with one. Carolina for preference. . . .

He looked at the house and grounds with a new interest as he approached. The future home of his evacuees. . . . The name, which he hadn't noticed before, was Bolsover Lodge. Quite a good garden for Lions and Tigers. Pity there were so many girls among the evacuees. He'd rather have had boys. Well, perhaps just one girl. . . . Carolina for preference. . . .

He walked up to the front door, slipped the envelope through the letter box, and set off homewards.

Arabella was waiting for him at his garden gate.

"Thought I'd come an' see how you're gettin' on," she said, fixing him with a suspicious stare. "Time *somethin'* was gettin' fixed up. They're plannin' to give some of 'em new shoes now. Time some of *us* had a look-in."

"Well, somethin' *is* fixed up, all right," said William, stung by this persistent persecution, "so you needn't come fussin' round here every minute."

"What's fixed up?" demanded Arabella, in no way relaxing her suspicious stare.

"I've got you 'vacuated," said William loftily.

"Where?" demanded Arabella.

"You'll see," said William. "I'll take you there when it's all fixed up."

"Thought you said it *was* all fixed up," said Arabella, pouncing unerringly on the weak spot.

"It is," said William, "but I can't let you go without me. I mus' take you there."

"When?"

"To-morrow."

"Why not to-night?"

"'Cause I can't get my things ready before to-morrow," snapped the goaded William. "Goodness, that ole Chamb'lain man took *days* gettin' things ready, an' you expect me to do it in about five minutes. I bet I've been a jolly sight quicker than what he was, anyway. I tell you, I can't take you till to-morrow."

"What time to-morrow?" persisted Arabella. "D'rectly after breakfast?"

"No," said William testily. "Goodness, I can't get everythin' ready by d'rectly after *breakfast*. I've gotter get a *bit* of sleep, haven't I? I can't go on 'vacuatin' people all day an' all night."

"You're not doin'," Arabella reminded him calmly. "You've only been doin' it for a bit of one day."

"Well, I'm jolly clever to've got it done in a bit of one day," said William, shifting the point of issue. "You can't say I'm not jolly clever to've got it done as quick as that."

"All right," said Arabella. "I never said you weren't, did I?" and added significantly, "*if* you've got it done. Can we go at eleven?"

"No, that's too early, too," said William. "I keep *tellin'* you it's too early."

"I *said* you'd never get it fixed up," said Arabella triumphantly. "I said so all along. I kept tellin' 'em so."

"Well, I *have* got it fixed up," snapped William, "an' you can come any time you like."

"Half-past eleven, then," said Arabella inflexibly.

"All right," agreed William, burning his boats behind him. "All right. Half-past eleven. . . . An' I *have* got it fixed up. I've been to the place an' wrote to it an'—an' got it all fixed up."

"Where is it?" said Arabella.

"I can't tell you," said William, realising that an inquisitive Arabella nosing about Bolsover Lodge would destroy any small hopes there might be of the success of the scheme. "They—they never tell 'vacuees where it is. They just take 'em there."

"All right," said Arabella. "You'll take us there at half-past eleven to-morrow morning. I'll go'n' tell the others now."

And, before William could gather his wits together to call her back and somehow wriggle out of the morass he had got himself into, she was gone.

"Oh, well . . ." he said philosophically.

He was always inclined to be a fatalist and to let things take their course. And he wasn't a boy to retreat, if he could help it, from any position he had once taken up. Better whatever catastrophe the evacuation scheme might lead to than a tame announcement of his inability to go on with it.

* * *

"William," said Mrs. Brown, looking out of the window the next morning at about eleven o'clock, "there's a whole crowd of children standing at the gate. I wonder what they want."

William paled. He'd had a wild hope that some fresh interest would have presented itself to Arabella and that she would have forgotten all about the evacuation project. Evidently that was not to be. He hadn't really thought it was. . . .

"I—I'll go'n' see," he said and went down to the gate, where he stood and gazed helplessly at the crowd. As he feared, it had been swollen far beyond its original number. He noticed Victor Jameson and George Bell. . . . It was a motley crew. Some of them had put on their oldest clothes, some of them their newest. Some carried parcels containing their possessions. All looked excited and eager. Arabella greeted him without any softening of her habitual grimness.

"We're ready if you are," she said shortly. "It's near enough half-past."

Maisie had evidently given up the struggle to wrest Arabella's position of leadership from her. She looked peeved and aloof, and her Queen Victoria features wore their "We are not amused" expression. Carolina fluttered her long eyelashes at him.

"You are clever, William," she murmured admiringly.

And once more that had to remain his sole comfort.

The evacuees chattered merrily on their way through Marleigh and Upper Marleigh. Not so their leader. He remained silent and aloof. He was wondering whether, when refused admittance to Bolsover Lodge, it would be better to take ignominiously to flight or to brazen it out. It wouldn't be easy to brazen it out. . . . He might pretend that there had been a "misunderstanding" (a word that, he had noticed, grown-ups always seemed to find useful) but he didn't think he'd get away with it. Not with Arabella, anyway. . . . Arabella was growing restive already.

"Where on earth *is* the place?" she snapped. "I don't b'lieve you've *got* one."

"I have," said William. "I jolly well *have*. . . . You wait!"

They had reached the gate of Bolsover Lodge now, and William's courage nearly failed him. It was, indeed, all he could do not to turn tail then and there and flee without excuse or explanation. But he never abandoned a cause till it was entirely lost. . . . So, with his spirits at zero, his heart somewhere in the pit of his stomach, he turned his dragging footsteps in at the gate, followed by his motley crew. . . . So slowly, indeed, did he walk that Arabella snapped:

"What's the matter with you? Have you gone *paralysed*?"

Carolina raised her blue eyes to the imposing structure of the house and murmured:

"Oh, isn't it lovely! William, you *are* clever!"

William smiled a ghastly smile and raised his hand to the bell. They heard it sound in the back regions. They heard slow footsteps approaching the door. The door opened and the old man in the green baize apron appeared. William, still poised for flight, tried to state his errand but, though he opened his mouth, his throat was so dry that no words came. To his amazement, however, no words were necessary. The old man was holding the door open to admit them.

"Come in, come in," he was saying. "Dear, dear! I'd no idea there were so many of you. I've done the best I could. I've done the best I could. . . ."

Dazed and stupefied, William entered, followed by his evacuees.

"Dear, dear, dear!" said the old man again, looking them up and down with peering short-sighted eyes.

"I'd no idea—— Who's in charge of you?"

"I am," said William, finding his voice at last and feeling that it must be a dream. He'd written the letter, of course, but somehow he'd never really expected it to result in this unquestioning welcome.

"I expected a grown-up," said the old man. He sounded resigned and apologetic. "Dear, dear! Well, well! . . . I've done the best I could. I hope you'll be comfortable. . . ."

And he began to show them round the house in the manner of a hotel proprietor trying to accommodate particularly difficult clients.

"This is the dining-room. Perhaps it would be better if you had meals in two sittings. There are rather too many of you to sit round the table all together. . . . Dear, dear! I shall have to get extra help in the house. If my niece were here she'd see to everything, but she's ill. She went into hospital the day before yesterday. It makes everything very difficult. Very difficult indeed. I'll do my best. . . . I'll do my best. . . . This is the morning-room . . . this the drawing-room. There's a big attic you could have for a play-room. . . . Now for the bedrooms. I'm afraid it will mean two in a bed and a mattress on the floor as well in some cases. Fortunately we have a lot of bedding. Major Hinton used to entertain a good deal before the war. . . . What about lunch? I can manage soup and stewed fruit. Would that do?"

The evacuees signified that it would. Carolina breathed "How lovely!" Maisie's regal features softened into what was almost a smile, and even Arabella, overpowered by her surroundings, raised no objection.

"I shall have to get extra help," said the old man again, as he shuffled his way upstairs. "I shall certainly have to do that. . . . I'd thought there would be more time to make arrangements. It's all come so suddenly. But I'll do what I can. . . ."

The bedrooms were large and numerous, and the idea of sleeping on mattresses on the floor appealed to the evacuees so much that each clamoured to be one of the favoured.

"Well, well," said the old man helplessly. "You must fix it up among yourselves. Dear, dear! It's all very difficult. But I'll do my best. . . . I'll do my best. . . .

"I SHALL HAVE TO GET EXTRA HELP," SAID THE OLD MAN
AGAIN, AS HE SHUFFLED HIS WAY UPSTAIRS.

Someone ought to have told me how many of you there
would be. Still, I'll try to manage. . . . I'll try to
manage. . . . Now, would you like to go into the garden
till lunch-time?"

The evacuees assented with enthusiasm. It was a
lovely day, and it was a lovely garden, complete with
trees, suitable hiding places, a pond, and an open stretch
of lawn. . . . The evacuees poured out joyously, with
shouts of excitement.

"Isn't it *lovely*!" said Carolina.

But Arabella was recovering her poise and gathering
her forces for attack.

"Where's the toys?" she demanded. "Where's the

new clothes? Where's the sweets? When's there going to be a party?"

* * *

The Committee of Residents for the Entertainment of Evacuees sat round the Vicarage table under the presidency of Mrs. Monks, reviewing their recent activities. On the whole, they considered that the evacuees had no cause for complaint. They were well-housed and well-tended. Toys and new clothes had been distributed, and parties had been given for them at regular intervals.

"Toby Weller wants another jersey," said Mrs. Monks. "He gets through them so quickly, I can't think what he *does* to them."

"Boys do get through things quickly," said Mrs. Brown with a sigh. "William's dreadful. . . ."

"Miss Milton has just finished another jersey," said Mrs. Jameson.

"I don't *think* we'll ask for that," said Mrs. Monks. "Her things are always such an odd shape. The one she did for Jimmy Foster wouldn't go over his head, but, as far as the rest of it was concerned, an elephant could have worn it. And that scarf she did for Polly Baker was about three yards long and came unravelled the first day. . . . Of course, she *means* well," she added hastily, remembering her rule to Believe the Best of everyone. "She means extremely well. It's only just that she can't knit, and, after all, knitting, like everything else, is a gift." She turned to Mrs. Parker. "You were knitting a jersey, weren't you, Mrs. Parker?" she said.

Mrs. Parker roused herself from a day dream.

"I'm sorry. . . . Oh, yes, I'm knitting one. I was just thinking about Georgie. He hadn't come in to lunch when I left. I've got no idea where he's got to."

"Oh, boys . . ." said Mrs. Jameson hopelessly. "They're dreadful. Victor hadn't come in either. I've given up trying to keep track of him. If he doesn't come in to a meal he just doesn't have it. And, after all, while he's out of the house, one does get a bit of peace. . . ."

"I know," sighed Mrs. Bell. "Boys *are* like that."

"My goodness," put in Mrs. Fellowes indignantly, "you talk as if girls were no trouble at all. Goodness knows where my Maisie is. She went out about eleven and I've not seen her since. And I wouldn't mind that so much if she hadn't put on her best coat. Heaven *knows* what it'll be like when she comes back. I never knew such a child for messing up her things."

"She can't be as bad as Ella," said Mrs. Poppleham. "She gets her things in such a mess you never saw. She's gone out in her best coat, too. I can't think why. When you *want* them to wear their best things, they won't, and when you don't want them to, they do. It's pure contrariness, I suppose."

"Carolina's gone to lunch with an aunt," said Mrs. Jones with a fond and complacent smile. "She looked so sweet in that green coat I made her and the hat to match."

"Yes, she looks nice in green," said Mrs. Poppleham, "and so does Ella. I sometimes think Ella's going to be quite nice-looking when she grows up."

"Ladies, ladies," said Mrs. Monks in her presidential voice, "what we're discussing now, please, is the evacuees. Do any of the others want anything besides Toby Weller?"

It seemed that they didn't. The committee looked faintly disappointed.

"I suppose we couldn't give them another party?" said Mrs. Fellowes.

"Hardly," said Mrs. Monks. "They had one last week."

"I wish we could do *something*," said Mrs. Popple-ham. "I mean—we've always had something on hand for them so far——"

At this moment Mrs. Monks was called away to the telephone. She returned a few moments later, looking tense and excited.

"It was old Cookham," she said, as she took her seat again. "You know, Major Hinton's servant. It seems that when Major Hinton went out to France he told old Cookham that he'd invited a second cousin of his in London to bring his family here out of harm's way if he wanted to. You know how vague the dear Major is. He said to Cookham, 'I believe he's got a pretty large family. I'm not quite sure how many.' Well, it seems that all the children have descended on him quite suddenly, and he's at his wits' end what to do with them. He says that there are more than a dozen. Probably Major Hinton told them to bring friends. . . . He would, you know. He's very hospitable. . . ."

"Didn't they give him any warning at all?" asked Mrs. Brown.

"Evidently a letter came the very morning of their arrival giving him no idea of the number or any time to make proper arrangements. I don't know whether the letter was really as vague as that, but, of course, his niece once told me that old Cookham can't write and can only just read. If she were there it would be all right because she's so very capable, but—poor old Cookham really isn't capable of coping with it alone."

"How many did you say were there?" asked Mrs. Brown.

"He says there are more than a dozen. . . . I don't

know whether there are *really* quite as many as that, but obviously something must be done about it."

"Poor little mites!" sighed Mrs. Jones. "When I think that one of them might have been my little Carolina. . . ."

"Yes," sighed Mrs. Fellowes, "or my little Maisie. . . ."

"You're right," agreed Mrs. Poppleham. "When one thinks of one's own dear children safe and happy at home one feels that one must do something to brighten the lives of these little waifs."

"They're not waifs exactly," objected Mrs. Monks.

"Waifs to all intents and purposes," said Mrs. Poppleham firmly. "Taken from their homes, bereft of a parent's care. I couldn't bear to think of my Ella without Mummy to turn to for everything."

"Well, ladies," suggested Mrs. Monks, "this really comes very opportunely. There is nothing more that we can do for our *own* evacuees at the moment, so I propose that we adopt the little strangers at Bolsover Lodge. From what I gather they are very badly equipped."

The committee brightened. Here was a fresh field for their energy, fresh scope for their organising ability. Their activities among their own evacuees had done little more than whet their appetites.

"Why not go over at once and see these poor children?" suggested Mrs. Monks. "We all have the afternoon free, I believe, and—well, it sounds as if the poor little things were urgently in need of help."

The suggestion was eagerly agreed to. The members of the committee were obviously champing to enter their new field of labour.

"I'll run home," said Mrs. Jones, "and get that brown coat of Carolina's. It's quite a good one, but she's grown out of it. It might fit one of them."

"And I'll get that pixie hood of Maisie's," said Mrs. Fellowes, not to be outdone. "She's got another. She doesn't really need it."

"I'll fetch one or two of Georgie's toys," said Mrs. Parker. "He must learn to give up to others less fortunate than himself."

"So must Ella," said Mrs. Poppleham. "I'll get one or two of hers."

"And I'll get that air-gun of Victor's," said Mrs. Jameson. "I'll be glad to see the last of it. He's broken two windows with it."

"And I'll take William's bow and arrow," said Mrs. Brown, stung to emulation. "Not that it'll do me any good. He'll only make another."

"Then, of course, there's the question of provisions," said Mrs. Monks. "Old Cookham said that he could manage lunch, but that he really didn't know what to do after that. We'd better take some cakes for tea."

"And I've got some tins of biscuits that I could bring," said Mrs. Miller. "I wish Freddie hadn't gone off like that. I'd have liked him to go with me and make friends with the little strangers. He'd have helped to make them feel at home."

"We'll call at Miss Milton's to collect any jerseys she has ready," said Mrs. Monks. "They're all right in an emergency. . . ."

* * *

As old Cookham opened the front door, a look of relief came over his face. There on the doorstep stood the members of the Committee of Residents for the Entertainment of Evacuees. They were laden with parcels. Mrs. Jameson carried Victor's air-gun together with two boxes of crackers that had been left over from Christmas. Mrs. Jones had Carolina's brown coat over one arm, the legless teddy bear in the other, and was carrying a bag of cakes. Mrs. Brown carried William's bow and arrows. Mrs. Monks carried a suitcase of miscellaneous clothing collected from various sources. Everyone carried something. . . .

"Well, here we are, Cookham," said Mrs. Monks brightly. "We've come."

"I'm very glad to see you, madam," said Cookham. "The young ladies and gentlemen are down at the bottom of the garden. A rare bunch, they are, too. Shall I call them?"

"No, we'll get tea ready for them first," said Mrs. Monks. "We're going to give them a really good tea just to cheer them up their first day. Then we can discuss future plans. Mrs. Simpkins here is coming to see to the cooking for this week at any rate. She's so kind and so efficient." Arabella's mother beamed kindness and efficiency from the back of the group. "And we've got a charwoman, and one or another of us will come over each day to see to things. . . . Gradually we'll get things into shape. Now leave the tea to us, Cookham. We'll see to everything. We thought that we'd have tea to-day in the nature of a party, so as to give the poor little things a really good time to start with. . . . Don't tell them. We don't want them to know till everything's ready. We want it to be a lovely surprise."

"Very good, madam," said old Cookham, "and glad I am to see you. A rare bunch, they are. . . ."

William and his evacuees had had an enjoyable afternoon by the pond. Arabella and some of the girls had made a "house" in the bushes, while the more daring spirits, headed by William and Victor Jameson, swung themselves right over the pond by a hanging branch. The process was not without its dangerous moments, and William had already fallen into the pond up to his waist, and Victor up to his knees. . . . Carolina, who was playing the character of the cook in the "house", kept forgetting her part and coming down to watch them.

"Oh, William, you are *wonderful*!" she said as William swung out into the middle of the pond and returned to (comparative) safety, dropping only one shoe on the way. Arabella, who had appropriated the part of mistress of the "house", also came down to the pond.

"When're we goin' to start havin' parties an' things?" she said.

"I can't do everythin' at once," said William, trying to draw his shoe back by means of a long stick. He'd enjoyed the afternoon but he foresaw difficulties ahead. One couldn't expect this dream-like state of things to last for ever. . . . He had a shrewd idea that the calm acceptance of their presence on the part of the caretaker was due to some mistake and that at any moment the dream might give way to stark reality. "I can't do everythin' at once," he repeated. "I've took a lot of trouble gettin' you a nice garden to play in, di'n't I?"

"Yes," agreed Arabella, "but what about tea? It's nearly tea time, isn't it?"

Obviously she was going to make herself a nuisance again.

"Oh, tea . . ." said William. "Yes, tea, of course. Yes, I'll have to fix up something about tea. I . . ."

It was at this point that they saw old Cookham coming across the lawn. So relieved was he to be rid of responsibility for his "rare bunch" that his air of bewilderment had vanished. He looked genial and expansive. He approached William, who had retrieved his sodden shoe and was engaged in ramming it over his sodden stocking.

"Tea's ready, young sir. Will you all come in to tea?"

The others had gathered round.

"Did you say tea?" stammered William. The dream was evidently to continue—for the present at any rate.

Old Cookham chuckled.

"Yes, and wait till you see it. Such a tea! Crackers and cakes and biscuits and presents. . . ."

Arabella gaped. . . . Like the Queen of Sheba there was no more spirit in her. And William on his side put on all the airs of a Solomon. He preened himself and plumed himself. He couldn't think where the tea had come from or why it had come, but for the moment it not only saved the situation but covered him with glory in the eyes of his followers.

"There's some nice ladies there to help serve it," went on Cookham. "Ever so kind, they are. They've brought toys with them and some nice new clothes."

William had long ago given up trying to understand what was happening. But it was in the right evacuee tradition. . . . Kind grown-ups doling out clothes and toys.

"Have they got a teddy bear?" said Carolina anxiously.

"Yes, little lady," said Cookham. "I saw that one of them had a teddy bear."

"Oh, good!" said Carolina.

"And one of them had an air-gun."

"Good!" said Victor Jameson. "I wanted a new one."

"And one had some bows and arrows."

"Bags me those," put in William.

"Is it a sort of party?" said Arabella. Her voice was low and humble—unlike her usual strident domineering tones.

"I should think it is!" said old Cookham.

William was recovering his poise.

"I thought it would be nice to have a party the first day," he said carelessly. "I didn't tell you about it 'cause I wanted it to be a surprise. . . . Well, come on. Let's go to it."

They accompanied him across the lawn—Arabella for once silent, so deeply impressed that her goggle eyes were almost falling out of her head, Carolina dancing along exultantly.

"Oh, William, you *are* clever. Oh, it was *lovely* of you

WITH GROWING HORROR—EVACUEES AND ENTERTAINMENT
COMMITTEE STARED AT EACH OTHER OVER BANKS OF
CRACKERS AND TOYS, SWEETS AND CAKES.

to think of the teddy bear."

They surged merrily across the lawn. They surged merrily through the french window into the dining-room. Then—with growing horror—evacuees and entertainment committee stared at each other over banks of crackers and toys and sweets and cakes. . . .

*   *   *

William walked disconsolately along the road.

"Well, they *asked* me to, din' they?" he muttered dejectedly. "They *wanted* me to. First they tell you to do what people ask you and then get mad when you do. Goodness, anyone'd think I'd murdered 'em 'stead of tryin' to give 'em a good time. 'S always the way. The more you try'n' help people the worse row you get into. . . . 'S'nough to make you never want to do anythin' for anyone all the rest of your life. Takin' all that trouble jus'——"

He stopped. Carolina was coming down the lane that joined the main road. She saw him and ran to join him.

"Oh, William, it was *lovely*!" she said.

"Lovely!" he echoed bitterly. "The end part wasn't lovely."

"It was for me," said Carolina. "You did it just right for me. You gave me a lovely afternoon, and then, just when I was beginning to want Mummy and my dear old teddy, you brought them along. Just like a wizard."

"Oh . . ." said William, slowly digesting this novel representation of the day's events. "Well, I bet you're the only one that thinks that. Gosh! You should've heard the way my mother went on at me."

"Mine went on at me a bit, too," said Carolina carelessly, "then she gave me threepence."

"Threepence!" said William relapsing into gloom.

"Gosh! Mine did the opposite. Seems to me, I'll never have threepence again the rest of my life."

"I'm going to spend it now," said Carolina.

"What you goin' to spend it on?" said William, interested despite himself, then, relapsing once more into gloom, "not that I'm int'rested in money. Not that I'm int'rested in *anythin*'! I'm jus' *sick* of people goin' on an' on an' on at me for nothin' at all. . . ."

"I thought I'd buy bull's eyes. I like bull's eyes, do you?"

"Bull's eyes?" said William, trying hard to retain his misanthropic attitude, his complete indifference to every aspect of life. "Well, yes. I don't mind bull's eyes."

"COME ON, LET'S RUN. . . . D'YOU LIKE BIG BULL'S EYES OR LITTLE ONES?" SAID CAROLINA.

"Come and help me buy some, William," said Carolina.

William brightened. Despite himself, interest in life was returning to him.

"All right . . ." he agreed. "I don't mind."

"And then let's divide them," said Carolina. "You have half and me have half. You've given me such a lovely day. Come on, let's run. . . . D'you like big bull's eyes or little ones?"

In a moment William was leaping along, whooping joyously.

Everything had gone wrong to-day.

Everything might go wrong to-morrow.

But bull's eyes still remained. . . .

Chapter 2

William Tries the Films

"They get over a hundred pounds a week," said Ginger.

"Crumbs!" gasped William. "A hundred *pounds*?"

"Yes," said Ginger, "a hundred pounds. I heard my aunt talkin' about it. Some of 'em get more."

"*More?*" said William incredulously.

"Yes, some of 'em get two hundred."

"They *couldn't* get two hundred," said William simply. "Not a *week*. No one could get two hundred *pounds a week*. Why, it's——" His mind grappled with the sum then gave it up. "It's ever so much money a day. They were pulling her leg."

"No, they weren't," said Ginger. "She knew a boy what got it. A boy what got two hundred pounds a week. Out in America, that was."

"Gosh!" breathed William. "A boy?"

"Yes, a boy. An' he got it for jus' actin' a boy in plays an' such like."

"Crumbs! I could do that," said William. "I bet I could act a boy in plays 's well as anyone. Did she tell you *how* this boy got doin' it?"

"Yes, she did," said Ginger. "She knew his mother. There's a man called a film producer what's at the head of it, an' this man called a film producer saw this boy actin' a boy in this play an' he said he could come an' act boys in his films an' this boy did an' he's still doin' it an' he gets two hundred pounds a week."

"Gosh!" said William again. "*Think* of it! You could buy sweets every day. You could buy——" Imagination boggled at the thought of what you could buy, and he could only heave a deep sigh and repeat, "Gosh!"

They walked for some yards in silence, then William said:

"If I'm ever one I'll get a real drum. The sort they have in bands. I've always wanted a real drum."

"Well, you aren't likely to be one," said Ginger. "How could you be? It was only 'cause this film man saw this boy actin' in this play that he got to be one."

"Well, I could get up a play an' act in it, couldn't I?"

"Yes, but you're not likely to have this film man comin' to watch you."

Even William had to admit the unlikelihood of this.

"There must be other ways," he said. "They can't all've got in it by bein' watched act in plays."

"No," admitted Ginger, "some go to him to act speshul. They've gotter have their faces yellowed."

"Yellowed?" said William in amazement. "Why?"

"It's jus' one of the rules," said Ginger vaguely. "Everyone what's on the films have got to have their faces yellowed. My aunt said so."

"But why?" persisted William.

"Well, I s'pose it makes it harder," said Ginger. "S'not easy actin' with a yellow face, so they make 'em have 'em yellow so's they'll try harder. The best ones are the yellowest," he went on, giving rein to his imagination, "an' the nex' ones the nex' yellow, and the ones what are jus' beginnin' have 'em jus' a little yellow, but they've all gotter be yellow. They won't let 'em act 'less they're yellow."

"They're not yellow in the ones you see at the pictures," objected William.

"N-no," agreed Ginger, and, unwilling to relinquish his position as an authority on the subject, added: "No, not the ones you *see*. They take off the yellow for the axhul *picture*. But while they're *actin'* they've gotter have it on. It's—well, it's jus' a sort of uniform. Jus' to show they're on the pictures. Same as policemen an' soldiers. It sort of shows they're on the pictures. They don't let 'em in 'cept they've got yellow faces. Same as a sort of pass word. . . ."

"They mus' look queer," said William thoughtfully.

"Yes, they do," agreed Ginger. "They look jolly queer."

"I wouldn't mind havin' a yellow face," said William, "if I got all that money. I wouldn't mind it, anyway. It'd be fun." He was silent for a few moments, then said: "Are there any of these film producer people in England?"

"Dunno," said Ginger. "'Spec' there are."

"I'd like to meet one," said William. "I could yellow my face all right. 'Spect they use crayons, don't they? Or paint. 'Spect paint's better. Crayon sort of drops off. An' I could act all right. I could say that piece we learnt out of Shakespeare or that play I wrote, called *The Bloody Hand*. It was a jolly good play. 'Spect I wouldn't start off with a hundred pounds a week. P'raps I'd start on twenty an' work up to it. I'd buy one of those big trumpets they have in bands, too, 's well as a drum. I'd have a jolly good time. . . ."

"Well, you're not likely to get a chance," said Ginger, and, despite William's glorious optimism, he was inclined to agree with him.

They had reached William's house now and, going

round to the kitchen garden, pulled up some carrots, washed them (partially) in the rain tub, and sat in the wheelbarrow munching them till the gardener came and drove them away. William would probably not have given another thought to his film career had he not, on going indoors, found his mother and Ethel discussing a forthcoming local pageant. They were seated at the morning-room table, Mrs. Brown intent on her usual task of household mending and Ethel intent on her usual task of sampling a box of chocolates from her latest admirer.

"It's going to be at Marleigh Court, after all," said Ethel, nibbling experimentally at the corner of a chocolate. "Miss Godwin's not keen, but she can't very well say 'no'. . . . Marzipan. . . . I wish I liked marzipan. . . . They say that her nephew's staying with her—Graham Godwin, the film producer, so perhaps he'll help."

William pricked up his ears. A film producer. Here was his chance. . . .

"I expect he'll be simply mobbed by people wanting jobs on the films," said Mrs. Brown.

Ethel laughed.

"They'll get no change out of him. Dorita Merton knows a girl who wanted a job on the films, and she wrote to him and he just wrote back to say that there were no vacancies. Then she went round to the film studios and the porter wouldn't even let her in. But Peggy Barlow knew someone he saw acting in a play and he gave her a job on the films straight away."

"I thought the pageant was going to be at Marleigh Hall," said Mrs. Brown.

"Well, Lady Markham's away just now," said Ethel, "and, anyway, Miss Tomlinson, the pageant mistress, insists on having it at the Court, because, though there's only a wing of it left now, it was the house where Queen Elizabeth stayed. Mrs. Bott was longing to have it at the Hall here, but Miss Tomlinson says it's impossible because the house is only nineteenth century."

"Dear, dear!" said Mrs. Brown placidly, hunting in her work box for a button for Robert's pyjama jacket. "I shouldn't have thought that mattered very much."

"Well, it wouldn't in a way," said Ethel, "only this Miss Tomlinson . . . Bother! Marzipan again! . . . They all seem to be marzipan. . . . Well, this Miss Tomlinson—coffee cream, that's better—she's a friend of Miss Milton's and she's spooky. All that lot are spooky. Anyway, she says that she can feel the influence of the old people that used to live in the house and that they help her. Give her ideas and that sort of thing. She says she has to have her pageant in a house that's the right period because of that."

"How very odd!" said Mrs. Brown. "I wonder if Robert would notice if I put a linen button on. I haven't got a pearl one the right size. . . . Who's going to be in the pageant?"

"Well, of course, I've got to be in it," said Ethel, assuming the bored air of the overworked local beauty. (William went through the motions of a bad sailor experiencing the worst results of a rough crossing, but Ethel ignored him.) "They consulted me, you remember, before they fixed on the date. Do have a choc, Mother. The oval ones are marzipan. It's very good marzipan."

"Thank you, dear," said Mrs. Brown, selecting a peppermint cream. "Will you be Queen Elizabeth?"

"Good gracious, no!" said Ethel, shocked by the suggestion. "The woman was definitely *plain*."

"Was she?" said Mrs. Brown vaguely. "I forget all

my history. I only remember that she walked on someone's coat in the mud. I always thought it so inconsiderate."

"She won the Armada," put in William, with an air of modest omniscience. He was kneeling on a chair, with his elbows on the table, playing with Mrs. Brown's mending materials.

"I don't care *what* she did, dear," said Mrs. Brown firmly. "I think it was most inconsiderate to walk on that poor man's coat. I can never think of her without seeing that poor man brushing away—and I'm sure he never got it off. I know what I've gone through with Robert's football shorts."

"Can I have one of your chocolates, Ethel?" said William in a conciliatory tone.

"You can have *one*," said Ethel generously, handing him a marzipan.

"Thanks awfully," said William.

"Nothing but boiling's any good at all," went on Mrs. Brown feelingly, "and I'm sure those coats they wore then wouldn't wash, much less boil. All that trimming and stuff. . . ."

"Can I have another, Ethel?" said William.

Ethel was a practical girl and saw a way of turning her dislike of marzipan to useful purpose.

"You can have all these," she said, picking out four oval ones, "if you'll go into the village and get my shoes from the cobbler's."

"A'right," said William. "Thanks . . ."

"William, do stop tangling up my darning wool," said Mrs. Brown, taking what was left of the ball from him.

"Sorry," said William, and added indistinctly through a mouthful of chocolate marzipan, "I'm goin' to be in this pageant thing."

"You're *not*!" said Ethel indignantly. "My *goodness*! Fancy *you* in it!"

"They *do* have children," countered William with spirit. "They had 'em in the last one."

"Yes," said Ethel, "and that's why they're not having them in this. That was the first thing they decided before even they thought of the subject."

William was non-plussed. He'd had a sudden glorious idea of appearing in the pageant and acting so well that the film producer should at once engage him for a film at a hundred pounds a week.

"Well, I think it'll be jolly rotten without children," he said. "I don't s'pose anyone'll want to see it without children."

"Oh, won't they!" said Ethel. "A lot more'll want to see it without children than with, let me tell you. They mess up everything they're ever in. When I think of that awful play at your school, when you——"

"Oh, that was a long time ago," put in William hastily. "I'm a jolly sight better actor now than what I was then."

"You messed up the whole thing," said Ethel.

"William meant well, dear," murmured Mrs. Brown, rescuing a set of linen buttons which William was absently detaching one by one from their card, and which had already acquired a greyish hue in the process.

"Meant well!" said Ethel, with a bitter laugh. "I never felt so ashamed in all my life. I——"

William decided to change the conversation by bringing the war into the enemy's camp.

"It's a jolly long way to the cobbler's, Ethel," he said, "and all the insides of those chocolates you gave me had the same taste."

"Well, I like that!" said Ethel. "I specially picked out

the best ones. Anyway, you'll have to go to the cobbler's now. You said you would."

"I know I did," said William, "but I'll make a better job of it if you'll give me another chocolate with a different taste inside."

"I'd take those I've given you back if I could," said Ethel severely.

"Well, you can't," said William, "'cept by cuttin' me open an' even if you did that you'd find 'em mixed up with a lot of raw carrots I've just et in the garden before I came in."

"Now, William," admonished his mother, "don't be vulgar. And stop sucking that reel of cotton. You'd better go to the cobbler's now. It's no good putting it off till you forget."

"All right," grumbled William, "if you want to get rid of me. Jus' a few measly chocolates, all with the same taste, for walking all the way to the other end of the village an' back. I've been paid as much as *twopence* for goin' as far as that, an' I bet those chocolates didn't cost a halfpenny. All right," dodging Ethel's avenging hand, "I'm goin' all right. . . . You needn't get mad." He secreted a small length of elastic from his mother's work box and slipped it into his pocket for future use as a catapult. "I might be a *slave* the way I'm treated," he went on pathetically. "Drove about without enough food to keep alive on. Drove miles an' *miles* just for a few chocolates, all with the same taste inside."

"Get along with you, William," said Mrs. Brown good-humouredly, and William got along with him, pausing by the open window on his way through the garden to say provocatively, "Well, I'm jolly glad *I'm* not goin' to be in that pageant if Ethel's bein' in."

But Ethel, instead of leaping through the window to

chase him down the garden as he'd hoped she would, pretended not to hear and went on discussing her pageant dress with Mrs. Brown.

William walked on to the cobbler's, his mind occupied by his film career. A hundred pounds a week. He'd give Ethel a big box of chocolates all with different insides just to make her feel how mean she'd been—though he couldn't somehow imagine Ethel ever feeling how mean she'd been. . . . But there were more difficulties in the way than he had realised at first. It had seemed at first quite simple to attract the notice of the film producer by a piece of magnificent acting in the pageant and thereafter to pocket his hundred pounds a week and purchase the drum and trumpet and anything else that appealed to him. He had even toyed with the idea of buying an elephant. . . . If he saved up for a month he might be able to afford one. It would be fun riding round the village on an elephant. And now it turned out he couldn't be in the pageant.

"Bet I c'n act as well as any ole grown-up," he muttered indignantly as he went down the two steps into the cobbler's small dark shop. "I could say that bit out of *The Bloody Hand* better'n any ole grown-up. 'Ah me! What cattastrophe is here? Gadzooks! Let us follow to his mountain lair and cut out his foul black heart. 'Tis the villain, the foul black Bloody Hand . . .' "

"Now then, now then, now then!" said the cobbler, looking up from his work. "None of that talk here!" He glared at William, whom he knew well. "And any of your tricks, you young limb, and——"

"Me?" said William with dignity. "I've come for my sister's shoes, that's all. I s'pose," with heavy sarcasm, "it's a free country an' people can come for their sister's shoes?"

"NOW THEN, NOW THEN, NOW THEN!" SAID THE COBBLER,
LOOKING UP FROM HIS WORK. "NONE OF THAT TALK HERE!"

"Free country indeed!" muttered the cobbler, reaching down a pair of very high-heeled shoes from the shelf and setting them on the counter.

William looked at the shoes with dispassionate contempt.

"Fancy a yuman bein' wearin' things like that!" he said. "If I was the King I'd stop 'em."

"Fine king you'd make!" said the old man.

"I bet I'd make a jolly good one," said William, "only I'm goin' on the films an' I can't do everythin'."

The old cobbler wrapped the shoes in a small piece of

newspaper, handed them to William, and returned to his work with an air of dismissal. William lingered in the doorway. He was a boy who liked human contacts and generally made the most of them.

"Guess how much she gave me for comin' along here for her shoes," he said.

The cobbler was hammering at a hobnailed boot and made no answer.

"I bet you're thinkin' she gave me sixpence, aren't you?" said William.

The cobbler continued to hammer as if William were not there.

"Thrippence, anyway, wouldn't you?" said William rather pathetically.

He waited in vain for an answer, then said:

"I bet you're thinkin' she gave me twopence."

The cobbler hammered away without speaking or looking up.

"Well, I'll tell you," said William, with the air of one reluctantly yielding to a passionate demand for information. "She gave me four chocolates, all with the same taste inside. What do you think of that?"

Still there was no response from the cobbler.

Piqued by the lack of interest, William went out, waited a moment, crept back, put his head round the door and shouted "Fire!" as loud as he could.

With unexpected agility the cobbler leapt from his stool, rounded his counter, and pursued William some distance down the lane. The hobnailed boot whizzed past his ear. William sped on till he'd reached a safe distance, then turned to watch the cobbler, having retrieved his boot, enter his shop again, still growling to himself . . .

Exhilarated by this little encounter, William walked

on, Ethel's shoes under his arm, his thoughts once more grappling with the problem of his film career.

The pageant was no use. It would be no use, either, evidently, to go to Marleigh Court and demand an interview with the man himself, for hadn't Dorita Merton's friend been turned away by the porter? He must think of some other way of impressing upon Mr. Graham Godwin his eminent suitability to be a film star. A hundred pounds a week! Gosh! He'd be able to buy that motor boat he'd seen in the Hadley toy shop last week. . .

He was passing a stile now, leading to a path across the fields, and he took Ethel's shoes from their wrapping of newspaper and placed them side by side on the bottom rung.

"Oh dear!" he said, in squeaky imitation of Ethel's voice. "However am I going to get up this great high stile?" He moved one shoe up in a sort of lunging leap. "Oh dear! Oh dear!" He moved the other one up to join it. "Oh dear! Oh dear!" He did the same with the next step, hugely delighted by the "imitation", which was actually as unlike his light-footed sister as possible. "Oh dear! Oh dear! I think I'll sit here a bit." He placed the shoes side by side on the top step but one. "I'll sit here and have a nice rest and a nice little think about how bee-utiful I am. Oh, I am so bee-utiful! I'm so bee-utiful that I'm goin' to be in the pageant. I'm the most bee-utiful girl in all the world. . . . I'll get down now." Again he moved the shoes, one by one, as if slowly and painfully, with squeaky ejaculations of "Oh dear! Oh dear!" till they reached the ground. "Oh dear! Now I've got to walk along in these awful shoes, but I mus' wear 'em 'cause I'm so bee-utiful."

Then, chuckling to himself, intensely amused by his own wit, he put them under his arm and walked along

the road again. This film business. . . . He must think of
a way. . . . The best thing would be to come on this film
producer man suddenly and start acting before he'd time
to get away. Then, of course, he'd see what a jolly fine
actor he was and ask him to come and act for him and
William would say, "All right. I'll come if you'll give me
a hundred pounds a week." (Even William's imagination failed to make this scene convincing, though it did
its best. . . .)

At this point he found that he had only one shoe of
Ethel's under his arm and had to go back several yards to
pick up the other. He threw it up in the air and caught it
again. He threw the other up in the air and caught it. He
remembered a juggler he had once seen and tried to
throw them both up in the air and catch them. He tried
several times without success, till finally each landed in
the ditch at opposite sides of the road. Fortunately one
ditch was dry. He emptied the water out of the other
shoe as best he could, put them both under his arm
again, and continued his homeward way. About this film
business. . . . Yes, he must somehow or other manage to
take this film producer man by surprise. . . . Out of
doors wouldn't be much good, because he might just
walk past him without taking any notice of him. No, he
must try somehow to get into Marleigh Court without
anyone knowing and then suddenly appear before this
Graham Godwin man and start acting. Take him by
surprise. That would be just the same as this man seeing
him acting in a play or in the pageant. But he'd have to
get his face yellowed first. . . .

A clod of earth hit him neatly over one ear, and,
looking round, he saw the face of Victor Jameson
grinning over the hedge in friendly invitation to a scrap.
William scrambled through the hedge and set off in

WILLIAM FOLLOWED VICTOR, HURLING ETHEL'S SHOES AT HIM ONE AFTER THE OTHER.

pursuit. Victor dodged through Hurst Farm yard. William followed, hurling Ethel's shoes at him one after the other, and catching him up in the main road. There they scuffled and wrestled, got each other on to the ground, and punched each other's heads till they were separated by a motor cyclist, who swerved violently to avoid them, narrowly escaped crashing into a tree, and left a stream of curses behind him as he righted himself and went on. The two boys rolled into the ditch, climbed out and walked on together, cheered and invigorated.

"Wish I'd heard some of those things he said prop'ly," said Victor wistfully. "They all sounded like new words."

"Jus' as if we were doin' him any harm!" said William indignantly. "It's a free country, isn't it? People can walk along the roads free, can't they? I wish I'd said that to him, but he went off too quick."

"My brother's bein' in the pageant," said Victor after a pause.

"So's mine," said William, "an' Ethel too."

"They're only havin' grown-ups this year," said Victor. "I don't care. It'll be rotten anyway. My brother can't act for toffee."

"Neither can mine. *Nor* Ethel."

"An' talk about *mean*!" said Victor. "I cleaned his motor cycle last week an' he wouldn't even give me a halfpenny. Jus' 'cause he said I'd got water in somewhere where it stopped it startin'."

"I know," agreed William fervently. "Guess what Ethel gave me for fetch——" He looked down at his empty arms. "I say, where are they?"

"What?" said Victor.

"Ethel's shoes," said William. "I was fetchin' 'em back from the cobbler's."

"You threw somethin' at me," said Victor, sending his mind back over the last ten minutes.

"Spect I threw 'em both at you," said William.

"Well, only one hit me."

"Well, that wasn't bad," William justified himself, "'siderin' you were runnin' about all over the place. . . . Anyway, where did it hit you?"

"On my arm. It only jus' touched me. An' I bet you weren't aiming at my arm, anyway."

"Bet I was," said William. "Bet I hit you jus' where I was aimin' at. But I meant, was it in the field or the road or where?"

"Farm yard, I think," said Victor vaguely.

"Let's go 'n have a look," said William. "She'll kick up an awful fuss if I go home without 'em."

An exhaustive search of the farm yard produced both shoes, one in a midden and the other in a trough of pigs' food. William inspected them anxiously and wiped them on his coat.

"Bet they'll be all right," he said. "I'll wipe 'em again when I get 'em home."

Slightly chastened, they walked for the rest of the way in comparative decorum, resisting all temptation to renew the scuffling match or use Ethel's shoes as missiles.

"There's a jolly fine cricket bat in a shop in Hadley," said Victor as they parted at William's gate. "I'd buy it if I'd got any money."

"You wait," said William mysteriously. "P'raps I'll be able to buy it for you."

Victor stared at him.

"You!" he said. "You've not got any money, either."

"I know I haven't," admitted William. "Not now, I mean. But I might have someday."

"Oh, so shall I, someday," said Victor airily. "I'm goin' to invent somethin' for makin' motor cars jump over things same as horses. I'd do it now, but I've not got enough money to buy the springs."

"Wait till I'm gettin' a hundred pounds a week," said William.

"Yes, I'm likely to wait," agreed Victor, as he set off down the road again.

William gave a short meaning laugh. (Why, he might be getting two hundred pounds a week by this time tomorrow!) and went indoors. Hiding Ethel's shoes under his coat, he crept upstairs to his room and rubbed them well, inside and out, with his bath towel. A faint aroma of pig food and midden still hung about them, but he took them into Ethel's bedroom and put them in the cupboard where she kept her shoes, right at the back, hoping, ever optimistic, that they would escape her notice till the smell had evaporated.

He met Ethel at the door as he was going out.

"I've brought your shoes, Ethel," he said meekly. "I've put them in your cupboard with the others."

"Oh, thanks," said Ethel, touched by his thoughtfulness. "If I find any more chocolates like those I gave you before perhaps I'll give them you."

"Thanks," said William, and could not resist adding: "P'raps it'll be me givin' 'em you nex' time."

She stared at him. He gave his short meaning laugh and went on to the garage.

For he had decided to begin his film career at once. Graham Godwin was at Marleigh Court, and he might as well get in before anyone else did. He had remembered that in a corner of the garage was half a tin of green paint left over from the painting of the garage door in the Spring. It wasn't exactly yellow, of course, but green and yellow were very much the same, and he remembered his mother's saying, when the painting was finished: "I don't think I like it much. It's such a *yellow* green."

He had decided to wait till he got to Marleigh Court before he actually put the paint on. He couldn't very well walk through the village with his face covered with green paint. At least, someone would be sure to try to stop him if he did. . . .

Slipping the tin of green paint under his coat, he set off in the direction of Marleigh. Everything seemed favourable to his exploit. Dusk was falling, and he met no one who knew him well enough to demand what he'd got there and what he was going to do with it and where he was going. He reached the gates of Marleigh Court unchallenged, entered them, and made his way cautiously round the house. All the downstair windows were in darkness except the library. Glancing through the curtains where they did not quite meet, he saw a man sitting in a leather arm-chair by the fire reading a book, and half a dozen or so women sitting round the table in the centre of the room. He recognised Miss Godwin, Mrs. Bott, Mrs. Monks, and Miss Milton. A tall intense-looking woman with deep commanding eyes and a deep commanding voice (she was addressing the meeting and had evidently been addressing it for some time) he took to be Miss Tomlinson, the pageant mistress. The man reading his book was evidently Graham Godwin, and the others were members of the Pageant Committee holding a meeting. Well, that was all right. It would give him time to put on his green paint, and then, when the meeting was over and they'd gone home, he could jump out at that Graham Godwin man and start acting. . . . The library happened to be particularly suitable for the manœuvre, because at the farther end of the room was a large window in a bay, which was shut off from the rest of the room in the evening by thick curtains. He went round to the bay end of the room, and, concealing himself behind a bush, began to put on his green paint. He'd had the foresight to bring the paint brush as well, but even so it was a more difficult process than he'd thought it would be. It was stiff and unwieldy. A lot went into his eyes and on to his hair, still more into his mouth and a certain amount on to his suit, but he managed it in the end. At least he covered the surface of his face more or less completely. It felt uncomfortable and tasted horrible, but William had never been the boy to abandon an enterprise because of a little discomfort.

The next thing to do was to get into the bay, of course. . . . He examined the windows. . . . One was a french window with a handle. He tried the handle. It was unfastened. Feeling slightly taken aback by the simplicity of the proceeding, he opened it, stepped silently into the bay, and closed it again softly. Then he stood still, and, holding his breath, listened apprehensively. But no one seemed to have heard him. On the other side of the curtain Miss Tomlinson's deep commanding voice continued its unremitting flow. . . . William put his head to the curtain to listen.

"And, of course," she was saying, "what I find most useful in organising these pageants is what I may call my—invisible assistants. The *influence* of the house. I don't mean that I actually count on any direct manifestation—though I have often experienced them—but I am conscious all the time of their—*inspiration*, shall I call it? They—*co-operate*. This house has re-echoed to the laughter of Queen Bess's ladies-in-waiting. . . ."

William moved the curtain a little in order to peep into the room. It was lit only by a standard lamp with a heavy old-fashioned frilled shade, and he didn't think anyone would notice. Yes, there they were sitting round the table—Miss Tomlinson at the head of it facing him, Miss Godwin at the foot with her back to him, the others at the side. And there was the film producer, reading by the fire. . . .

"To the laughter of Queen Bess's ladies-in-waiting," repeated Miss Tomlinson. "Well, as the old philosophers teach us, nothing ever really dies. *Something* of them is here still, and——"

She broke off, staring fixedly at the aperture in the curtain through which William had been peeping. The others followed the direction of her gaze, but William had hastily withdrawn.

"Is anything the matter, Miss Tomlinson?" said Miss Godwin.

Miss Tomlinson roused herself with an effort. She wore the air of one who is entrusted with some weighty secret.

"Nothing, thank you, Miss Godwin," she said. "Nothing that you—well, nothing. What was I saying? Oh yes. One's *unseen co-operators*. A sudden inspiration about a dress, a gesture, a sudden insight into a motive. Where do they come from? Where——?"

Again she stopped, staring at the aperture through which William had again incautiously peeped. Again the others looked round, to see only the curtain behind which he had quickly withdrawn. Again Miss Godwin said:

"Is anything the matter, Miss Tomlinson?"

And again Miss Tomlinson had replied in a portentous voice:

"Nothing, nothing, Miss Godwin. Nothing that—well, nothing," and continued: "It's all a matter of sensitiveness to atmosphere, of course. What one can hear and see and feel, another can't. What to one is a thin veil is to another a thick wall."

"How long will the pageant take?" said Miss Godwin, stifling a yawn.

Miss Tomlinson looked at her a little reproachfully.

"I shall be coming to that in a moment, Miss Godwin," she said. "The practical matters are quickly settled. It's the atmosphere that is important. Unless one can feel that one is in sympathy with the atmosphere, or rather that the atmosphere is in sympathy with oneself——"

At this moment William, who was wondering whether Mr. Graham Godwin would prefer an exhibition of tragedy or comedy, peeped through the curtain again in order to take a look at him, and once more met the eyes of Miss Tomlinson. Once more the fount of Miss Tomlinson's eloquence dried up. This time, however, instead of summoning all her forces to recover it, she turned her eyes slowly to Miss Godwin and said, in the deep commanding voice:

"Is this house haunted, Miss Godwin?"

"Oh dear, no," said Miss Godwin cheerfully. "No one's ever seen or heard anything of a ghost here. No rattling chains or headless men or anything like that."

Miss Tomlinson threw her a quelling glance.

"That," she said ominously, "is as it may be. . . . The fact is that the influence of this house is *not* friendly to us."

"Oh, Miss Tomlinson!" chorused the ladies of the committee, glad of an opportunity of taking a part in the proceedings at last. "Why?"

"The influence of this house," said Miss Tomlinson, her voice now so deep that it seemed to arise from the ground at her feet, "is definitely *un*friendly to us."

Miss Milton looked round nervously. Mrs. Monks said: "Really, Miss Tomlinson!"

Mrs. Bott said: "Well I never! Fancy that!"

Miss Godwin yawned outright and said: "Pray explain."

"Yes," said Miss Tomlinson, as if coming to a sudden momentous decision, "I will explain. I *must* explain. . . . While I have been sitting here I have had one, two, three," she counted conscientiously, "yes, *three* separate manifestations of an unfriendly influence."

Graham Godwin from the fireside threw them an exasperated glance and turned over a page of his book.

"What exactly did you see or hear?" said Miss Godwin.

"My mother was a seventh child," murmured Miss Milton.

"I'll tell you," said Miss Tomlinson again. "*Three* times I saw an—apparition."

"Of what?" persisted Miss Godwin.

"A bodiless head," said Miss Tomlinson, speaking each word slowly and distinctly. "A—bodiless—head. It *hovered* three or four feet from the floor. It was indescribably malevolent. It appeared quite suddenly and as suddenly disappeared. Three separate times!"

"I saw nothing," said Mrs. Monks.

"Nor I," said Miss Milton.

"Of course you didn't," said Miss Tomlinson crushingly. "The message was not for you. It was for me. It was a challenge. There are hostile forces at work here. Evil influences." She turned dramatically to her hostess. "Miss Godwin, I cannot hold the pageant here."

Miss Godwin brightened.

"I'm sorry to hear that, Miss Tomlinson," she said.

"I am convinced," said Miss Tomlinson, "that if I attempted to do so in face of the warnings I have just received, some terrible disaster would ensue." She turned to Mrs. Bott. "Is your offer to place the Hall at my disposal still open, Mrs. Bott?"

"Yes, of course it is," said Mrs. Bott. "Botty an'

me'd be ever so pleased. Why, Botty's gone and bought a history book for it special."

"You *do* understand, don't you, Miss Godwin?" said Miss Tomlinson in sepulchral tones. "I have had experience of such things. I *dare* not disregard such a warning."

"Of course I understand," said Miss Godwin, trying to hide her relief. "I take it then that the meeting is at an end?"

"The sooner the better," said Miss Tomlinson, throwing a slightly apprehensive glance at the curtain. "As far as I am concerned, I do not feel safe for a moment under a roof where this has happened. . . . May we meet to-morrow at this time at the Hall, Mrs. Bott?"

"Oh, yes," said Mrs. Bott, smiling happily. "Botty'll be ever so glad. He nearly got a prize for history once when he was a boy. He'd've got it if he hadn't muddled up Nelson with Nero, or some such names."

Miss Godwin rose from her seat.

"Well, then . . ." she said in a voice of finality.

The meeting rose and went into the hall. The sound of their voices was heard, first in excited discussion and comment, then in farewells. . . . The front door closed on them. They passed the window on their way down the drive.

"The plainest manifestations I've ever had," Miss Tomlinson was saying. "That green light, of course, has a special psychic significance . . . indescribably evil. . . ."

"My mother was a seventh child," Miss Milton was saying again.

Miss Godwin returned to the room.

"What a *relief*!" she said to her nephew. "I was

beginning to wonder how on earth I was going to endure it."

"So was I," said her nephew. "The manifestation was certainly a godsend."

"And what a *fool*!" said Miss Godwin with a laugh. "Manifestation indeed! It was pure imagination and nothing else."

"Of course it was," said her nephew.

"Well, I'll go upstairs and rest till dinner time," said the old lady. "The whole thing's been rather a strain."

Her nephew opened the door for her and closed it softly behind her. He stood there till she was out of earshot, then went across to the curtains, drew them back, grabbed William by the neck and dragged him into the room.

"Now, you young rascal!" he said. "What d'you mean by it?"

"Hi!" said William. "Stop squashin' my neck in. I want to *act*. Lemme go. I want to *act*, I tell you." He wriggled himself free, struck an attitude and began, in a hoarse unnatural voice: "Ah me! What a cattastrop is here! Gad zooks! Let us follow to his mountain lair an' cut out his foul black heart. 'Tis the villain, the foul black . . . I forget what comes next," he went on, returning to his natural voice, "but I can do Shakespeare, too. Listen. I'm doin' Shakespeare now." He struck another attitude. "Friends, Romans, Countrymen, lend me your ears. My ears are in the coffin here with Cæsar for Brutus——"

Mr. Graham Godwin was staring at him in amazement.

"What on *earth* have you got on your face?" he said.

"Paint," answered William simply. "It's green 'cause

"WHAT ON EARTH HAVE YOU GOT ON YOUR FACE?" SAID
MR. GRAHAM GODWIN.

I hadn't any yellow. Green's as good, isn't it?" he asked
anxiously.

"It depends what its purpose is," said Mr. Graham
Godwin.

"For goin' on the films, of course," said William
impatiently. "I can get yellow when I'm doin' it prop'ly.

This is just to *try* with . . . jus' sort of to *show* you. I don't mind not gettin' a hundred pounds a week straight off. I don't mind workin' up to it gradual."

"What on earth are you talking about?" said Mr. Graham Godwin.

"Well, you're the film man, aren't you?" said William.

Light dawned on Mr. Graham Godwin.

"Oh, I see," he said. "No, I'm afraid I'm not. Nothing so exciting. That's my cousin. We've got the same name and we are rather alike in appearance, so people are always confusing us. I'm sorry you've been misinformed. . . . I'm merely a hard-working business man who was hoping for a fortnight's quiet fishing here. When I found that the place was to be invaded by that pageant bunch, I—well, I'd better not try to describe my feelings to a young child like you. I'm sorry for your disappointment, of course."

"Fishin'?" said William with interest. "Where d'you fish?"

"In the river on Sir Gerald Markham's estate."

"I once tried there," said William bitterly, "an' a man came along an' nearly killed me."

"Yes, of course," said Mr. Godwin mildly. "It's preserved, you know. I have to pay quite a handsome sum for it." He studied William with a dispassionate interest. "I say! You look pretty awful."

"I feel pretty awful," admitted William. "It's makin' me feel sick, too. It feels like claws somehow, clawin' at you when you try speakin' or smilin'. Clawin' at you all the time, come to that. Can't think how anyone *axe* in it. Gosh! I'd be bein' sick all the time. I bet it kills 'em off pretty quick. No wonder they've gotter pay 'em such a lot of money."

"There's some turpentine in the stable," said Mr. Godwin, "and I'll get some hot water. We'll soon have it off. But—look here!" He glanced round in a conspiratorial fashion. "I don't want my aunt to know about this."

"About what?" said William.

"About you and your green paint. I want her to go on thinking it was the old fool's imagination. You see, she's a very conscientious woman, and she might think it her duty to give them the real explanation of the mystery, and then they might all come trooping back, and that doesn't bear thinking of, does it? How did you get in?" William pointed to the curtain. "Let's go out that way, then. We can get round to the stable without meeting anyone. . . . Come on."

They went together through the curtain, out of the french window and round the house in the darkness towards the stable.

"I'll be jolly glad to get it off," said William indistinctly. "It seems to get worse an' worse. I think it's sort of *soakin'* into me."

"Never mind," said Mr. Godwin. "We'll make short work of it when we get to that turpentine," and added casually: "Would you like to come fishing with me to-morrow?"

William stood still and stared at him incredulously.

"D'you mean—real grown-up fishin'?" he said.

"Yes, of course," said Mr. Godwin.

"Crumbs!" said William on a note of ecstasy. "Real grown-up fishin'. . . ."

How often had he watched his father and Robert set off for it on holidays and begged unsuccessfully for permission to accompany them! How often had he set off alone, with stick, string and bent pin in puny unconvincing imitation of them. And here was the real thing being offered him. A career on the films—never very real even to his vivid imagination and now connected inseparably in his mind with the taste and feel of paint and the sensations of physical nausea—faded into nothingness in comparison. Real grown-up fishing. . . .

"Crumbs!" he said again. "I should think I *would*!"

"All right. Come round for me to-morrow morning. I'll take a picnic lunch for us both. . . . Here we are. Now let's get to work. . . ."

Half an hour later William set off homewards. Traces of green paint still hung about him, but his appearance at least now suggested that of a human being.

Ginger was hanging over his gate waiting for him.

"Whatever've *you* been doing?" he greeted him.

William brought out his great news.

"I'm goin' fishin' to-morrow."

"I thought you were goin' on the films."

"Oh that!" said William, taking his mind back with an effort from the glittering future to the dim past. "I gave that up ever so long ago. It's jus' like claws clawin' at you, an'—*Gosh*, doesn't it make you feel sick!"

Chapter 3

William and the Bird Man

It was Henry's mother who, without realising it, suggested the idea.

"I really think that people ought to do more for the evacuees," she said. "Not a thing's been done for them lately."

She spoke idly without considering the effect of her words. She didn't even know that William was listening to her. Certainly it didn't occur to her that he might take matters into his own hands and try to do something for the evacuees.

"We've gotter do something for the evacuees," he said sternly to his Outlaws that evening. "Nothin's been done for 'em for ever so long."

"They did enough for 'em at Christmas," said Ginger.

"Yes, but they wouldn't let us help," complained William. "Stopped us every time we tried to give 'em a good time. Gave 'em a party an' then wouldn't let 'em have a good time."

Their minds went back to the Christmas party given by the residents to the evacuees. It had had the makings of a good party, but, just as the Outlaws were succeeding in working up what seemed to them the right spirit, Authority had stepped in and accused them of "getting rough". They had been ignominiously ejected from the Village Hall in the middle of a game invented by William, called Lions and Tigers, in which the evacuees were joining with zest and which had already shown the weak spots in the party clothes hastily put together by kind-hearted but unskilled residents.

"They say that they could hear the noise at the other end of the village," said Mrs. Brown sternly to William when the affair had been reported to her.

"Well, that only shows they were enjoying themselves," said William. "You can always hear the noise at the other end of the village if people are enjoying themselves."

"I can enjoy myself without being heard at the other end of the village," said Mrs. Brown.

"Yes," admitted William, "but I don't call enjoying myself what you call enjoying yourself. An'——"

"Now that will do, William," said Mrs. Brown.

Once William had suggested to the Outlaws the idea of having a party of their own for the evacuees, in which grown-ups should have no hand, it became more and more attractive the more they thought about it.

"An' we'll play Lions an' Tigers an' Germans an' English an' P'lice an' Outlaws, jus' as much as we like without any ole grown-ups messin' about an' stoppin' us, an' I bet it'll be a better party than the rotten ole one they had at the Village Hall. Why, more'n half of 'em went home with their collars on. I jolly well don't call *that* much of a party."

The first thing to be decided was where to hold the party. The obvious place, of course, was the old barn, but the last few weeks had shown it to be so far from weatherproof that even the unquenchable spirits of the Outlaws shrank from the prospect of a party held in such a downpour as the holes in the roof were capable of supplying. They thought over the various outhouses and sheds that adjoined their own houses, but none seemed capable of accommodating a gathering of such a size as the proposed party.

"I bet they'll *all* want to come," said William complacently, "when they know we're goin' to have Lions an' Tigers again. They went crazy over that game. The one what wore that jersey what ole Miss Milton knitted got *all* the stitches dropped by the end. She'd dropped half to start with while she was makin' it. I bet they'd go *anywhere* to play it again."

But still the question was—where?

"That Wing-Commander Glover what's at Marleigh Aerodrome's gotter big stable behind his house what he doesn't use," said Ginger. "Couldn't we get him to lend it us jus' for the party?"

"He's nuts on Ethel, isn't he, William?" said Henry. "Couldn't you get her to ask him?"

They looked hopefully at William, and William tried to look like a boy in whose hand lay the key to the whole situation. Actually his influence with both Ethel and her admirer was negligible. Certain of Ethel's admirers tried to win their way into her favour by making much of the little brother, but Wing-Commander Glover did not belong to that class. Wing-Commander Glover was tall and thin and had a somewhat languid manner and a monocle, but, despite the languid manner and the monocle, he was no fool, and he had realised from the first that the way to Ethel's heart did not lie through William, and therefore wasted no time or money in that direction. He even followed her example in treating him as if he didn't exist. William found this disconcerting (generally speaking, he made a good thing out of Ethel's admirers), but it did not damp his optimism.

"All right," he said airily. "I'll have a talk with him. I bet he'll let us have it all right. I bet if I have a talk with him he'll let us have it. . . ."

It happened that he ran into Wing-Commander Glover on the way home. Wing-Commander Glover had been paying a call on Ethel, and his eyes held a far-away look that vanished as soon as they fell upon William. William turned and began to accompany the Wing-Commander towards Marleigh.

"You been to see Ethel?" he said conversationally.

"Yes," said the Wing-Commander shortly.

"She's jolly fond of you," said William with what he took to be consummate tact. "Jolly fond."

His companion made no comment.

"I bet she likes you better than what she likes most of 'em," went on William and added, as the Wing-Commander still made no comment, "I *bet* she does. A *jolly* sight better."

His companion continued to make no comment.

"I bet there's lots of 'em she doesn't like as much as what she likes you," William assured him emphatically. "I've often heard her say she met you in the village an' so on."

The Wing-Commander adjusted his monocle and broke his silence.

"Don't let me take you out of your way," he said with pointed politeness.

"Oh, no, that's quite all right," said William. "Quite all right. I'm goin' home to tea soon as I've finished talkin' to you."

"DON'T LET ME TAKE YOU OUT OF YOUR WAY," SAID
THE WING-COMMANDER WITH POINTED POLITENESS.

"Good-bye, then," said the Wing-Commander suc-
cinctly. "I'm sure you want your tea."

"Oh, no, I'm not in a hurry," said William. "I don't
mind waitin' a bit. I told you Ethel was jolly fond of you,
didn't I? Well"—William considered that by now the
way had been sufficiently paved and with characteristic

directness plunged at his objective—"well, will you lend us your stable for a party we're goin' to have?"

"Certainly not."

William, though taken aback, did not give up the struggle.

"It's for the evacuees," he explained. "It's goin' to be a jolly good party."

The Wing-Commander made no response.

"I once heard Ethel say you were jolly good looking, except for your nose," went on William. "At least, I *think* it was you she said it about. . . . Or it might have been except for your chin or that glass thing you wear in your eye. . . ." He paused hopefully for an answer but, getting none, continued: "Won't you lend us your stable? We'll take jolly good care of it."

"Certainly not," said the Wing-Commander again. "Good-bye."

He quickened his pace and left William staring after him nonplussed. He considered that he had conducted the interview with superlative finesse and couldn't think what had gone wrong with it.

"He mus' be deaf," he muttered as he turned to wend his homeward way. "He couldn't 've heard any of those things I said. Deaf, that's what he mus' be. Abs'*lutely* deaf."

He was tempted to assume that had the Wing-Commander heard his request he would have granted it, and therefore to take his permission as given, but a certain gleam in the monocled eye told William, who was an expert in such matters, that its owner was not to be trifled with, so he reluctantly abandoned the idea.

"He was jolly sorry," he reported to the Outlaws that evening (for he did not like to admit that his influence with Ethel's admirers was less than they thought it was), "he was *jolly* sorry he couldn't let us have it, but it doesn't b'long to him. It b'longs to his landlord. He *wanted* to let us have it, but he was afraid of bein' put in prison if he did."

The Outlaws were perfectly satisfied with this explanation. Each, indeed, formed the mental vision that William meant him to form—of a humbly apologetic Wing-Commander flattered by William's request.

"Well, now," went on William hastily, lest any breath of reality should dispel the pleasant dream picture, "we've gotter think now what to try next. We can't have it in the ole barn an' we can't have it in that man's stable. Where else is there we could have it?"

"There's that cottage on Marleigh Hill behind the aerodrome," suggested Henry. "It's got a big studio place in the garden. That artist with a beard used to have it but he's gone now."

"Good!" said William. "If it's empty we can just take it without askin' anyone."

"It's not empty," said Ginger. "I heard someone tellin' my aunt about it. A man what's writin' a book about birds has taken it. He goes about watchin' 'em, an' takin' photos of them an' suchlike, but he doesn't use that studio place at all."

"I bet he'd let us have it, then," said William optimistically. "Stands to reason he would, if he's not usin' it. . . ."

"You go'n' ask him," suggested Douglas.

"No, it's someone else's turn," said William. "I asked Wing-Commander Glover for his stable."

"Well, you jolly nearly got him to let us have it, didn't you?" Henry reminded him.

"Oh, yes, I did," agreed William hastily. "A'right,

I'll go'n ask this bird man. I bet I'll get him to let us have it all right."

Actually, despite his failure over the matter of the stable, William was quite anxious to try his hand again. Thinking the matter over, he had come to the conclusion that he had sprung his request too abruptly. He should have taken longer in leading up to it. He should have made a friend of the Wing-Commander and identified himself with his interests before he even mentioned the stable. . . . He decided to make a friend of the bird man and identify himself with his interests. . . .

He set off early the next morning to begin the process. He made his way to the cottage—a small picturesque affair with a thatched roof called Hillside Cottage—and knocked tentatively at the door. He had decided to open fire by asking the way to Marleigh and then lead the conversation as best he could to birds. No one answered his knock, however, so he made his way cautiously round to the back. No one seemed to be about. The studio had been built in the back garden by a former owner of the cottage and was a solid fair-sized building, with large windows and ample sky-light. William walked round it and looked in at the windows. There were a few packing cases lying about, but otherwise it was empty. His spirits rose. . . . It was just the place for his eva-cuees' party. An obviously watertight roof, plenty of room for Lions and Tigers and no neighbours to be disturbed, for the cottage stood alone on the hillside. A pity the bird man wasn't in. William felt loth to return home without having begun his task. He went to the front door and knocked again. Still no reply. Cautiously he crept up to the window near the front door and looked in. A small room, with a writing-table just under the window, a lot of photographs of birds and things lying about on it, a bookcase full of books. From where he stood William could see some of the titles . . . *Birds of the British Isles*, *Birds of the Tropics*, *Birds* . . . *Birds* . . . *Birds* . . . Gosh! He must know a jolly lot about birds. He turned reluctantly from the door and looked about the empty hillside. Probably the bird man was somewhere there studying birds. He'd go and have a look for him. Better than going home without even having started on his well-thought-out plan. . . . He wandered about for some time without meeting anyone and was just giving up the quest when a man seemed suddenly to arise from a bush a short distance from the path. He wore blue spectacles and was slipping a pair of field-glasses into his pocket.

"Hello," said William pleasantly.

"Hello," answered the man shortly.

He looked about forty and had a suave expressionless face with a long straight mouth.

"You the bird man what lives at Hillside Cottage?" said William conversationally.

"Yes," said the man. "My name's Redding."

William, remembering the Wing-Commander's reception of his request, checked his impulse to ask at once for the loan of the studio. He was not a boy to whom indirect methods made any great appeal, but he had decided to take at least a day paving the way on this occasion and he was going to stick to his decision.

"I'm jolly int'rested in birds myself," he said, "but I don't know much about them."

"Really," said the man.

He was taking up a sort of rucksack from the bush. William caught sight of a small camera in it.

"You been takin' photos of 'em?" he inquired.

"I do when I get the chance," said the man. "They aren't easy to photograph, you know. It means hours of patient watching and waiting."

"I was jus' wantin' to meet someone what knew about birds," said William in his most ingratiating manner. "I'm *jolly* int'rested in 'em. An aunt of mine's gotter bird-table an' she gives 'em crumbs an' things. All my fam'ly's int'rested in birds. I'm always tellin' off our cat for killin' 'em. An uncle of mine sometimes sends us grouse an' things from Scotland. We're *all* int'rested in birds. I don't think there's a family in England more int'rested in birds than what we are."

"Indeed," said the man.

William sighed. It wasn't proving easy to establish such relations as would almost automatically result in the loan of the studio. He tried again.

"I 'spect you know every bird there is, don't you?" he said, increasing the effusiveness of his manner.

"Yes," said the man.

He had strapped up his rucksack and was preparing to set off down the path towards the cottage. At that moment a bird alighted on the bush beside them, stayed there a few seconds, then flew off.

"What bird was that?" said William, delighted at this opportunity for further bird discussion.

"An ousel," said the man.

"Goodness, I've always been interested in them," said William. "An' I've always wanted to know a bit more about them. Do they stay in England all the winter?"

"Yes," said the man.

William searched desperately in his mind for another intelligent question and was rewarded by further inspiration.

"Where do they build their nests?" he asked.

"In tall trees," said the man.

"I sort of thought they did," said William, playing for time while he tried to think of something else to ask.

"Er—what are their eggs like?" he said at last.

"A sort of greyish white," said the man. "Not very interesting. Good-bye."

And with that he strode off down the path towards the cottage.

William stood looking after him. He had done his best, but on the whole he hadn't been very successful. . . . He'd tried to identify himself with the man's interests, but he couldn't truthfully say that he'd made a friend of him. He didn't like to leave matters thus in mid-air. . . . He wandered slowly down the path to the cottage. There was no sign of Mr. Redding. He must have gone inside. Well, he'd just go and have another look at the studio, anyway, and see what other games they'd be able to play besides Lions and Tigers. They might be able to have a jolly good game with those packing cases—Storming the Fort, or something like that. He went round to it and looked in at the window again. Yes, there were enough packing cases for a jolly good game of Storming the Fort. He went back to the cottage and inspected it wistfully. He'd have liked to get on better terms with its occupant before going home. He hadn't done too badly, he assured himself (he'd certainly been emphatic enough about his interest in birds), but he didn't feel that he'd put their relations on a footing of real friendship, as he'd meant to. He'd make one last effort. He must think of something else to ask him about the ousel. . . . what it lived on or something like that. And while he was answering he'd try to think of something else to ask him. And so on. . . .

He was at the back of the house, and the back door was ajar. No use going round to the front and bothering the man to come to the front door and open it to him. Better just go in at the back in a friendly way without bothering anyone and ask his question about the ousel.

He pushed open the back door and stepped into a small tidy kitchen. He went through it and, opening another door, found himself in the sitting-room that he had seen through the window, with the writing-desk and book-cases. The man was sitting at the writing-table at work on a complicated diagram. He swung round as the door opened and something flashed into his face that made William—he didn't know why—want to turn and run for his life. It vanished so quickly that William thought he must have imagined it, and the face beneath the blue glasses became once more bland and expressionless.

"I jus' wanted to ask you somethin' else about that ousel," he explained. "I told you I was jolly int'rested in birds, didn' I?" He approached the table and looked down with interest at the diagram the man was working on.

"What're you drawin'?" he asked with interest.

The man tapped the diagram carelessly with the tip of his pen.

"This is the diagram of a blackbird's lungs," he said. "I'm writing a book at present on wild birds' diseases."

"Corks!" said William. "I didn't know they had any."

"No, few people do," said the man. "It's a subject that is very difficult to investigate and that few people have studied thoroughly. Consumption of the lungs isn't at all uncommon in wild birds, nor is cancer, nor the other diseases we suffer from ourselves."

"Crumbs!" said William. "Fancy that! Do they have stomach-ache, too?"

"I believe so."

"Gosh! I'm jolly sorry for them, then. I've had it an' it's rotten."

William took up the diagram to study it more closely and uncovered another one underneath.

"What's the other one?" he asked.

"That," said Mr. Redding, "is the diagram of a sparrow's stomach."

"Corks!" ejaculated William in an awestricken voice. "It doesn't look as if it could get inside a sparrow."

"It's on a large scale, of course," said the man, drawing both diagrams gently but firmly from William's hands. "And now I'm afraid I must ask you to go. I have a lot of work to get through this morning."

William, rather to his surprise, found himself outside the closed door with nothing to do but walk down to the gate. On the whole the second interview had been more successful than the first. Apart from the curious moment at the beginning that by now seemed so fantastic as to be quite unreal, Mr. Redding had been friendly and expansive. He'd talked quite pleasantly about wild birds' diseases and blackbirds' lungs and sparrows' stomachs. William wondered how soon it would be before he could approach the subject of the loan of the studio. Perhaps to-morrow. . . . He'd go round to see him again first thing to-morrow morning. He'd have to think up something else to ask him, of course. Then he stopped short. In the excitement of looking at the diagrams, he'd forgotten to ask him what ousels lived on. Pity to have gone to all the trouble of thinking the question out and then not to have used it. He could easily think something else out for to-morrow. He turned and retraced his steps to the cottage. It would be interesting to see what the man was doing now. Making more diagrams, perhaps. . . . They were jolly interesting, those diagrams. . . . He'd like to have another look at them. He'd liked the sparrow's stomach particularly. Gosh, fancy all the ole worms it ate gettin' down into a place like that! They wouldn't know what to make of it after livin' in ordin'ry holes in the earth. P'raps they'd be all chewed up, though, an' wouldn't know anythin' about it. Had birds got teeth? He'd ask Mr. Redding. It'd make a good question for to-morrow. He'd use the one about what ousels lived on to-day, and save up the one about had birds got teeth for to-morrow.

He opened the garden gate and walked up the little path to the front door. A thick bush hid the window from him. He put his hand on the knocker then drew it back. He'd just take a peep through the window first and watch Mr. Redding doing his diagrams. He'd like to know how they were done. He might try doing them himself, once he'd got the hang of it. He crept round the bush to a point where he could see into the room without being seen. Yes, the man was still at work on a diagram. He had a note-book open, and there were a few photographs scattered around. Suddenly he collected them all together, put them into a large envelope and moved out of sight. William's bump of curiosity was an abnormally large one. He couldn't resist craning his head a little further round the bush to see where the man had gone and what he was doing. He gazed with eyes that opened wider and wider. . . . The man had taken up two or three bricks from the floor and was putting the envelope into the hole thus made. Then he began carefully to replace the bricks. At that moment the church clock struck one, and William realised that he was already late for lunch. Reluctantly he turned and went away. . . . Jolly good idea, he thought, keeping

THE MAN HAD TAKEN UP TWO OR THREE BRICKS FROM THE FLOOR, AND WAS PUTTING THE ENVELOPE INTO THE HOLE.

those diagrams and things under the floor, then they'd be all right if there was a fire. There'd been a fire down at Hadley the other day and a lot of papers and stuff in a lawyer's office had been burnt. Probably Mr. Redding had heard about this and had decided to keep his diagrams of birds' stomachs and things somewhere where they'd be all right if a fire broke out. It was a jolly good idea. He'd see if he couldn't get some of his own bedroom floor up and keep a few of his own most important things there. He decided not to go back to Hillside Cottage after lunch. He wasn't going to rush the thing. He'd noticed that grown-ups generally got fed up with him if they saw a lot of him. He'd never been able to understand it, but there it was. . . . He'd wait till to-morrow and then he'd go and ask him what ousels lived on. Then after an interval he'd go and ask him if birds chewed, and after another interval the time should be ripe for asking for the loan of the studio. . . .

He joined his Outlaws for the afternoon, and, in the course of a thrilling game of Red Indians, gave them a somewhat rose-coloured account of his negotiations with Mr. Redding.

"Oh, yes," he said carelessly, "he thinks he'll be able to let us have it all right. He *thinks* he'll be able to let us have it. We had a jolly int'restin' talk about birds this mornin'. About sparrows' stomachs an' things. He *thinks* he can let us have that studio place, but he's not quite sure yet. He's goin' to let us know in a day or two. He was jolly int'rested in a bird I found called the ousel, an' he told me all about sparrows' stomachs an' things. . . ."

On going home for tea he was somewhat disgusted to find Wing-Commander Glover there and still more disgusted to find his father. . . . One didn't get much chance to talk with a visitor present, but one got no chance at all with one's father. . . . He made a few attempts to enter into conversation but after the third parental, "That's enough, William," resigned himself to a silent meal. When tea was nearly over, however, the same bird he had seen that morning fluttered suddenly on to a bush by the window.

"That's an ousel," said William, unable to resist the opportunity of showing off his newly acquired knowledge.

His father and the visitor turned to look at it.

"It's a nuthatch," said the Wing-Commander.

"Of course it's a nuthatch," said his father. "What on earth made you think it was an ousel?"

William was disconcerted for a moment then made an effort to recover his prestige.

"Well, I know a jolly lot about an ousel, anyway," he said.

"What do you know?" challenged his father, in whom savoury sandwiches and a second cup of tea were combining to induce a slightly more genial mood.

"I know a jolly lot," said William importantly. "I know that it spends the winter in England and that it makes its nest in tall trees and that its eggs are a sort of greyish white."

He looked round complacently, enjoying his brief moment of triumph.

It was very brief.

"On the contrary," drawled the visitor, "the ousel is a migratory bird, it nests in heather and holes in the wall, and its eggs are blue-green, speckled with red."

William stared at him indignantly.

"Well, I bet you can't draw a sparrow's stomach," he said.

"I have no desire to," answered the Wing-Commander.

"An' I bet——"

"That's enough, William," said Mr. Brown.

William relapsed once more into silence. It was an indignant, resentful silence. Someone had been pulling his leg, and it wasn't the airman or his father. One glance at Wing-Commander Glover was enough to tell you that he was incapable of pulling anyone's leg, and his father definitely wasn't in a leg-pulling mood this afternoon. It was the bird man who had been pulling his leg. He must have known quite well that the bird wasn't an ousel. One only had to remember the piles of bird books, the field glasses, the camera, and the complicated diagrams to realise that. No, the bird man had been pulling his leg. And William didn't like having his leg pulled. Not by comparative strangers, anyway. In that case, self-respect demanded that the leg-puller's leg should be pulled in return before normal relations could be resumed. He'd have to pull the bird man's leg before he went on with the studio campaign. . . . He didn't know how he'd pull it yet. He'd have to have a good think during the night. He'd be sure to get an idea of some sort. . . .

He slept, as usual, too soundly to have much time for thought, but the idea came to him as he was dressing the next morning. He'd take that diagram of a sparrow's stomach out of the hole in the floor and put an old exercise book or something like that in its place. That'd jolly well pull his leg. Then they could start square again and go on with the studio business. But honour must be satisfied first. William had never yet let a leg-pull go unrequited. . . .

A search in that nightmare medley of allsorts that

filled the drawer in which William kept his personal possessions revealed an ancient arithmetic exercise book, freely adorned with capital Ws in red ink, as were all William's arithmetic exercise books.

It would be a good joke to put that in place of the diagram of the sparrow's stomach. . . . The bird man wouldn't know what on earth to make of it. In order further to mystify his victim, William tore off the green paper back that bore (in detail and many times repeated) his name and address. That'd be a jolly good leg-pull. He'd go to get his diagram of a sparrow's stomach and find only an old exercise book without a name. He wouldn't know what to make of it. . . . William chuckled to himself as he put the exercise book into his pocket and set off to Marleigh Hill.

As he neared the cottage, he saw the bird man coming out of the gate, his rucksack on his back, and making his way along the path that wound round the hill. William dodged behind a bush and waited till he was out of sight then cautiously approached the cottage. It was obviously empty. He tried the front door and the back. Both were locked. A small window, however, just above the sloping scullery roof was open. William, who was an adept at effecting entries by unorthodox means, climbed a drainpipe, scaled the roof and inserted himself through the small open window with almost incredible agility. He found himself on a landing. A flight of stairs led down to the front door. Holding his breath, prepared for instant retreat through the window and down the drainpipe if necessary, he slowly descended the stairs. No one was about. He entered the little sitting-room. There were the rows of bird books on the shelves . . . the writing-table by the window . . . the brick floor. . . . It took him a little time to find the loose bricks, but, once he had found them, it was the work of only a few seconds to take out the diagram and put the exercise book in its place . . . then return by way of the sloping roof and drainpipe, the diagram safe in his pocket. Still no one was about. The hill around him was deserted, and the only sound was the hum of an aeroplane just leaving the aerodrome below.

On reaching home, he found Ethel alone in the morning-room. He took out his diagram with a flourish.

"Like to see a pitcher of a sparrow's stomach, Ethel?" he said, handing it to her.

Ethel wrinkled up her delicate nose and assumed an expression of acute nausea.

"How disgusting!" she said, turning her head away. "How absolutely *disgusting*! Take the thing away! Mother," as Mrs. Brown entered, "William keeps showing me disgusting pictures of things' insides. I wish you'd stop him."

"Don't do it, William," said Mrs. Brown automatically.

"And he's not washed his hands or brushed his hair since he got up," went on Ethel.

"Go and wash your hands and brush your hair, William," said Mrs. Brown, taking up her basket of household mending.

"The way he goes about is *awful*," went on Ethel vehemently. "I saw him in the village this morning and he looked *awful*. His shoes were undone and his stockings were coming down. He must have used his garters for catapults or something again."

"Had you, William?" asked Mrs. Brown.

"They're all right now," said William, looking down at the offending garments. "I've tied 'em up with string."

"Had you used your garters for catapults?"

"Well, I *needed* a catapult," explained William evasively, "an' then I lost it an' had to use the other one, too. I bet it's somewhere in the old barn. I bet I can find it if I have a good look."

"That's another penny off your pocket-money," said Mrs. Brown firmly. "I've told you not to use your garters as catapults. Now go and wash your face and brush your hair."

"Mean ole tell-tale," muttered William as he went up to the bath-room. "Mean ole tell-tale, that's what she is. . . ."

The idea of getting even with Ethel in a mild way grew in his mind as he plied sponge and brush in a half-hearted absent-minded fashion. Having successfully, as he thought, got even with the bird man, it would be child's play getting even with Ethel. Yes, he jolly well *had* got even with the bird man. He chuckled to himself as he imagined him going to his hole for his diagram of a sparrow's stomach and finding only an old exercise book.... His hand went to his pocket and he fingered the paper affectionately. He'd put it back to-morrow. Seemed a pity, though, to have taken all that trouble getting it and then not to be able to make any use of it. . . . He went thoughtfully down to lunch.

"What are you doing this afternoon, Ethel?" asked Mrs. Brown.

"I'm going to a *thé dansant* at the Grand Hotel in Hadley with Wing-Commander Glover," said Ethel in what William called her put-on voice. "It's a one-eyed hole and a *dreadful* floor, but it's the only possible place round here."

"Re-ah-ly?" mimicked William in his best imitation of the put-on voice, conveying a forkful of cabbage to his mouth with ostentatious elegance.

"Be quiet, William," said Mrs. Brown, and:

"Oh, shut up," said Ethel.

But an idea had just occurred to William—an idea so neat that he almost choked over the mouthful of cabbage. He'd kill two birds with one stone. He'd get even with Ethel and make some use of the diagram he had so cleverly purloined. He'd slip the "disgusting" diagram of a sparrow's stomach into Ethel's bag, then, when she was having tea with Wing-Commander Glover at the Grand Hotel, and talking in her put-on voice, she'd open her bag to powder her nose and find it there, and it would make her as mad as mad. And even if she got in a bait and tore it up, it wouldn't matter. The bird man could easily draw another, and, anyway, he wouldn't know who'd taken it. . . .

* * *

"It's a rotten floor, of course," drawled Wing-Commander Glover, adjusting his monocle.

"Absolutely rotten," agreed Ethel languidly, as she leant back in her chair and sipped her tea elegantly.

"But interesting to watch the natives."

"Frightfully interesting," said Ethel, trying to look as little like a native as possible.

"Some pretty frightful dancing, isn't there?"

"Frightful," said Ethel, with an air of aloof disgust.

"An awful crowd, too."

"Awful," agreed Ethel, with a world-weary smile.

"Well," said the Wing-Commander, "shall we tread another measure or are you tired?"

"Oh no," said Ethel, trying to strike the happy mean between readiness to tread another measure and lofty amusement at the whole affair.

"Quite amusing, these little local shows," said her escort, preparing to rise.

"Quite," said Ethel.

But she felt that the combined effect of the hot tea and the hot room had brought an unbecoming sunset glow to the alabaster whiteness of her small and usually exquisite nose, and opened her bag to take out her powder compact.

"What on *earth*'s this?" she said, unfolding a paper, then flushed and hastily folded it up again. That *wretched* boy putting his disgusting pictures of animals' stomachs into her bag! She'd speak to her father about it as soon as he came in to-night. . . . But her companion had seen it, too. The monocle dropped from his eye and the colour faded from his sunburnt cheeks.

"May I see that, please?" he said.

"Certainly not," said Ethel with spirit. "It's nothing at all. I don't know how it came to be in my bag."

The Wing-Commander was staring at her in incredulous horror. He looked like a man in the throes of a nightmare.

"Give me that paper," he said again.

"Certainly not," said Ethel angrily, ramming the paper back into her bag.

Throwing chivalry to the winds, he snatched the bag out of her hands, opened it, and took out the paper.

"If you want to know what it is," said Ethel with dignity, "it's the diagram of a sparrow's stomach. I"— she wasn't going to let him know that William had played the trick on her—"I'm interested in sparrows' stomachs. It's—it's a sort of hobby of mine."

The Wing-Commander's face was still a mask of incredulous horror.

"Is it yours?" he asked.

"Of course it is," said Ethel, "and I can't think why you're behaving in this ridiculous way about it."

"Who drew it?"

"Well, actually," said Ethel, "my little brother drew it. He's—interested in sparrows' stomachs, too."

"Do you expect me to believe that a child of that age drew this?"

"I don't care what you believe," said Ethel. "I've never been treated so rudely in all my life and I'm never coming out with you again."

"I don't think you are," said the Wing-Commander grimly.

Throwing chivalry still further to the winds, he took her by the arm and propelled her firmly to the door. She found herself in his car driving beside him down the road at a breakneck pace.

"It's ridiculous," she said hysterically, "for a great man like you to get upset by a little thing like the drawing of a sparrow's stomach. I didn't like it myself. I told William that it was disgusting. I didn't know he'd put it in my bag. But to behave like this about it. . . ."

They had reached the house now. In grim silence the Wing-Commander walked up to the front door accompanied by Ethel. William was in the hall, putting on his coat. The Wing-Commander, his face still pale and set, confronted him with the drawing.

"I found this in your sister's possession," he said. "She says that you drew it."

"Oh, that sparrow's stomach thing," said William easily. "Well, it was this way——"

But at that moment Mr. Redding appeared at the open front door. His face, too, was pale and set. William had torn off the back of his exercise book, but had forgotten that every other page in it was freely adorned

"I FOUND THIS IN YOUR SISTER'S POSSESSION,"
SAID THE WING-COMMANDER.

with his name and address. Mr. Redding had come to invite William up to the cottage and there to find out by fair means or foul what had happened to his diagram.

"He's the man that drew it," said William, pointing to Mr. Redding. "He's writing a book on birds' diseases. He's jolly clever at 'em."

Mr. Redding took one look at the Wing-Commander, tall and threatening in his Air Force uniform, and shrank back instinctively. The Wing-Commander took one look at Mr. Redding and stepped forward. Then the surprising thing happened. Ethel was struck motionless with

"OH, THAT SPARROW'S STOMACH THING," SAID
WILLIAM EASILY.

amazement as the airman pursued Mr. Redding down the road, leapt upon him and pinned him to the earth. Not so William. Ever since he could remember he'd wanted to dial 999. He went into the morning-room and dialled it.

"Please send a policeman along at once," he said

importantly. "Wing-Commander Glover's gone mad. He's killin' people all over the place."

* * *

"Well, you see," said William to an entranced audience of his Outlaws, "I saw this man drawing the thing through a window, and I knew it was a drawing of an aeroplane, all right, so I watched to see where he put it an' then I waited till he'd gone out of the house and took it. I didn't tell any of you about it 'cause I knew he might kill me an' I knew that if he knew you knew he'd kill you too. I couldn't take it straight to Wing-Commander Glover 'cause I knew this man was watchin' me, so I put it in Ethel's handbag when she was goin' out to tea with him so's he'd see it an' get it back an' know that a spy was spyin' on his aerodrome. . . ."

He stopped a minute and, as it were, listened to himself. It sounded all right. It sounded even better than he'd thought it would. Now he came to think of it, it really *had* happened like that. . . .

With increasing confidence, with a wealth of gesture, with a growing faith in his own heroism, he continued his story. . . .

Chapter 4

William and the Unfair Sex

William wandered disconsolately down to the beach. His family had come to the sea for their summer holiday, and so far (they had arrived the day before) William was not amused. His father had set off for the golf course directly after breakfast. Robert and Ethel had joined a tennis set in the hotel garden. Mrs. Brown was sitting in the lounge, learning the art of "quilting" from another visitor and thinking how nice it was not to have to think about lunch. William had spent an enjoyable half hour experimenting first with the lift and then with the revolving doors, and had finally been forbidden to use either unattended. An electrician was now at work on the lift, and the old gentleman who had been carried round the revolving doors six times in William's whirlwind wake had been with difficulty persuaded not to sue the management for damages.

"No one stops *them* enjoying themselves," muttered William. "*They* go about havin' a good time all the time, but the minute I start they all get mad at me."

The absence of other children at the hotel added to his grievances.

"Lot of sick'nin' ole grown-ups," he muttered. "Lot

of sick'nin' ole grown-ups with nothin' to do 'cept talk newspaper stuff an' stop other people havin' a good time. Nice sort of holiday with a lot of sick'nin' ole grown-ups who——"

He stood looking down at the beach and his gloom increased. It was a sunless chilly morning and only two little girls were there.

"*Girls!*" he ejaculated scornfully. "Rott'n ole *girls*! Sickenin' ole grown-ups an' rott'n ole girls! You'd think there was a sort of *famine* of boys. You'd think someone'd killed 'em all off. . . ."

His first thought was to walk away in disgust, but the little girls were about his own age and were in any case preferable to the grown-ups at the hotel. He watched them uncertainly. . . . They were dressed alike in grey skirts and white blouses, and they were both hunting for shells, which they put into cardboard boxes, yet, despite the similarity of their clothing and pursuits, they worked at opposite ends of the beach and never spoke to each other. Slowly William went down the short sloping path to the beach. There he pretended to be deeply interested in the rocks and seaweed at the foot of the cliff. One of the little girls drew nearer in her search for shells till she was within hailing distance. Then she stood upright and said: "Hello."

William started and looked at her as if seeing her for the first time. He frowned as if interrupted in a pressing matter of business.

"Hello," he said distantly, and turned to study the cliff face again with an air of expert knowledge, pulling out bits of loose rock, examining them intently, then putting them back again.

The little girl watched him with interest, then said: "What are you doing?"

William, who hadn't the faintest idea what he was doing, did not reply. Instead he countered aloofly: "What are *you* doing?"

"I'm collecting shells," said the little girl, holding out the cardboard box. "Look."

William looked. Yellow shells, blue shells, white shells, black shells. It was an impressive collection. But William carefully maintained his pose of bored detachment as he said:

"What are you collectin' 'em for?"

The little girl's face shone suddenly.

"For Miss Twemlow," she said on a note of deep reverence.

"I'M COLLECTING SHELLS," SAID THE LITTLE GIRL, HOLDING OUT THE CARDBOARD BOX.

"Who's she?" said William.

"Our form mistress," said the little girl on a note of still deeper reverence. "She's set us a holiday competition."

"And is that what your sister's doing, too?" asked William.

The little girl's expression changed from reverence to an almost venomous hatred.

"My sister? *That* awful girl? She's not my sister. I hate her. I'll never speak to her if I can help it."

"Then why have you got the same clothes on?" demanded William.

"It's our school uniform," said the little girl bitterly. "I *hate* going about in the same clothes as that awful girl, but it's the school uniform. She goes to the same school an' she lives here, too. I've begged and *begged* my mother to get me different clothes to wear in the holidays so that I needn't look the same as that awful girl, but she won't."

"Why don't you like her?" said William.

The little girl's face grew tense.

"It's because of Miss Twemlow," she said. "She used to be my best friend before Miss Twemlow came to the school. But last term she played the meanest trick on me. The meanest trick I've ever heard of."

"What was it?" said William with interest.

The little girl lowered her voice confidentially.

"Miss Twemlow had promised to let me sit by her at the half term lecture. She'd *promised*. . . . I was having a music lesson just before and couldn't get in till just before the lecture began, and Angela—she's that awful girl—*knew* that Miss Twemlow had said I could sit next her, and she went and sat next her and wouldn't move when I came. Miss Twemlow never remembers who she's promised, and it's a matter of honour with us to let the one she promised first sit there."

William was silent for a moment, digesting this startlingly novel aspect of school life. On the few occasions on which he had sat next to a master at a lecture it had been because he had been forcibly dragged there from the seclusion of the back row, where his activities were proving a rival attraction to the lecture itself.

"Crumbs!" he said at last. "It mus' be jolly different at a girls' school."

"And it's not the first time she's played a trick like that on me," went on the little girl indignantly. "You can't trust her an inch. . . . Not an inch."

She stared across the beach at the other figure in grey skirt and white blouse that was wandering to and fro, occasionally stopping to pick something up from the sand.

"Is she gettin' shells now?" asked William.

The little girl's expression grew yet more tense.

"Yes. She's in Miss Twemlow's form, too. And Miss Twemlow's quite nice to her—I can't think why, because she's an awful girl. An *awful* girl! But, of course," the ferocity of the little girl's expression softened to one of rapt and languishing sentimentality, "Miss Twemlow's so kind she'd be nice to anyone, however awful they were. She's so kind. And so beautiful." The little girl's expression was by now one of fatuous imbecility. "She's the most beautiful person who's ever lived. And clever, too. She can read things in the original language and that sort of thing. And she's got the most beautiful voice. In 'God save the King' you hear it above all the others. Just like an angel. She *looks* like an angel, too. I used to think Miss Folkat was an angel, before Miss Twemlow came, but—well, there's no comparison. Miss Twemlow's—well, I should think she's *more* beautiful than an angel. . . ."

William listened with growing bewilderment, feeling vaguely glad that such emotional tangles did not complicate the simple lawlessness of his own school life.

"In a way," the little girl was saying, "she's like Norma Shearer, but in a way she's more beautiful. Do you know what I mean?"

William, however, was tired of discussing the unknown Miss Twemlow. He looked at the collection of shells and said:

"How many have you got?"

"Nearly two hundred," said the little girl proudly. "I keep them at home, of course. These are just the ones I've found to-day." She looked across at the other little girl and said wistfully: "I'd love to know how many Angela's got."

"Why don't you ask her?" said William.

"*Ask* her?" repeated the little girl, registering exaggerated horror and disgust. "Good gracious! I wouldn't ask her *anything*. Not if I was dying. Not after the way she behaved over that concert. I've not spoken to her since, and I wouldn't—not if she went down on her bended knees and begged me to. . . . I say, I wish you'd go and ask her. Don't say it from me, of course. Just ask her how many she's got. Just as if you wanted to know yourself. You needn't stay with her, of course, because she's an *awful* girl."

"All right," said William, who was becoming rather bored and wanted to see what the other little girl was like. "I'll go an' ask her how many she's got."

"Yes," said the little girl anxiously, "and see if she's got an orange one. I can't find an orange one. Plenty of yellow, but not orange, and I know people *do* find orange ones here. Don't tell her I want to know, of course. Just find out if she's got one. I'm trying to find a blue stone, too, to have it polished and made into a brooch for Miss Twemlow. She's got blue eyes. She——"

But William, feeling that he couldn't bear to hear any more about Miss Twemlow for the present, was setting briskly off to the other little girl at the farther end of the beach. He slackened his pace as he neared her, wondering how to introduce himself, but she forestalled him, raising an earnest face from her search to say:

"What's your name?"

"William," said William. "I know yours. It's Angela."

She looked exactly like the other little girl, except that she was dark whereas the other little girl was fair.

"You've been with that *awful* Adela," said Angela, with a note of severity in her voice. "Don't believe anything she says. She's the most *awful* story teller. I don't know how you could *bear* to speak to her. She used to be my best friend, but that was before I really knew her. She played me the meanest trick!"

"What did she do?" said William.

"She found Miss Twemlow's places in chapel when it was my turn. She missed her turn with having a bilious attack, but that wasn't my fault. She knew Wednesday was my day, and when I went to find the hymns and lessons in Miss Twemlow's place she'd found them and put in the markers and she couldn't deny it because Lucy Masters *saw* her doing it. Have you ever *heard* of a meaner trick?"

William, who had heard of several, said nothing, and the little girl continued:

"I haven't spoken to her since, and I won't. I

wouldn't speak to her not—not even if the end of the world came. She knows why, too. She must have about the guiltiest conscience of anyone in the world. Wednesday's been my day ever since Miss Twemlow——"

"Yes," interrupted William. "She told me all about her."

"She doesn't *know* about her," said Angela passionately. "Miss Twemlow's only nice to her out of kindness. Miss Twemlow's so kind that——"

"Yes," said William hastily, "she told me all about that, too. How many shells have you got?"

"Nearly two hundred," said Angela. "How many has she?"

"Nearly two hundred," said William. "Have you got an orange one?"

"Has she?" said the little girl warily.

"No, have you?"

"No," admitted Angela. "I've got heaps of yellow ones, but I can't find an orange one anywhere. I know there are some, 'cause someone found one here. . . . Will you help me look?"

William considered. He did not find either Adela or Angela stimulating company, but there didn't seem anything else to do.

"Well . . ." he said vaguely.

"I'll tell you a *wonderful* thing Miss Twemlow once did——" began Angela, but William interrupted.

"No, thanks," he said firmly. "I don't want to hear anythin' more about her. Tell you what. The other one—Adela—wants an orange shell, too, so I'll go off an' look for one an' if I find it, you can toss for it. How's that?"

Angela looked a little sulky.

"All right," she said, "if you won't look for me."

"Well, she wants one, too," said William, "so it's quite fair."

"All right," said Angela, thinking it was better than nothing, "but if you give it to *her* I'll never forgive you."

"I'll give it to the one the toss comes to," said William. "The first one, that is. An' I'll give the next to the other. I bet I find lots."

He took up his position conscientiously between the two of them and began to look for shells. Those he found he divided and took half each to his new friends, with apologies for the absence of an orange one.

"I bet I find one nex' time," he said. "I'm jolly good at findin' things."

If he'd found one he'd have left the little girls altogether and betaken himself to more congenial pursuits, but he was a boy who never liked to abandon any project unfinished. He'd undertaken to find an orange shell and he meant to do it. . . . Moreover, as time went on, a sort of zest seized him. He found ten shells, twenty, thirty . . . and, though he still didn't find an orange one, Adela and Angela were separately very grateful to him for his contributions. The only drawback was that all topics of conversation led with a sort of diabolical fatality straight to Miss Twemlow and her perfections. . . .

Going to bed that night, he decided that the whole thing was a waste of time and that in future he would avoid both Adela and Angela and their shell-hunting ground.

"As if I'd got nothin' else to do," he muttered to himself indignantly, "but look for orange shells!"

As a matter of fact, however, he *had* nothing else to do, and the next morning, after an unsuccessful attempt to explore the kitchen regions of the hotel, out of which he was chased by a temperamental Italian chef, he turned his feet slowly and almost reluctantly in the direction of the beach. He determined to find two orange shells and to reconcile Adela and Angela. They both liked talking about Miss Twemlow, so it would be much better for them to talk to each other about her than to him. He wasn't interested in Miss Twemlow. He imagined her, in fact, as a mixture of Violet Elizabeth Bott and a Pantomime Dame. But he quite liked Adela and Angela, in spite of their limited conversational powers, and wanted them to be able to talk to each other about Miss Twemlow. He thought they'd enjoy it. . . . Now that they wouldn't let him experiment with the lift or the revolving doors or explore the kitchen, there seemed nothing to do but find an orange shell and reconcile Angela and Adela. He'd never reconciled anyone before and it would be a novel experience. . . . The morning, however, was unsuccessful. He didn't find an orange shell and he didn't reconcile Adela and Angela. He took his "finds" to each in turn as he had done the previous day and put in a certain amount of not very subtle reconciliation propaganda, which did not enhance his own popularity.

"Wouldn't you like to talk to *her* about Miss Twemlow?" he said to Adela. "*She* likes talkin' about her, too."

"*Her!*" ejaculated Adela fiercely. "I'm never going to speak to her again. I've *sworn* it. And Miss Twemlow can't know her as I do or *she* wouldn't speak to her, either. Haven't you found an orange shell yet?"

"No," said William, "not an orange one. I keep finding other colours."

"Has *she* got an orange one?"

"Why don't you go an' ask her," said William, "an'

have a nice talk about—about Miss Twemlow an'
things?"

"Never!" said Adela dramatically, and, pleased with
the effect, repeated, still more dramatically: "*Never!*"

Angela was just as uncompromising.

"Speak to her! What should I speak to her about?"

"Miss Twemlow," suggested William.

"Speak to *her* about Miss Twemlow?" said Angela
fiercely. "Why, Miss Twemlow——"

"All right," said William, returning to his no-man's
land to look for an orange shell.

If it hadn't been for the orange shell he certainly
wouldn't have gone down to the beach again after lunch,
but he wasn't going to be beaten by a little thing like an
orange shell. Moreover, all the other members of his
family had gone out, refusing to take him with them, and
an old gentleman, roused from his after-lunch nap by his
whistling, had been so disagreeable that William felt
there was nothing for it but to go down to the beach
again. No one seemed to want him but the little girls.
Perhaps the little girls didn't exactly *want* him, but at any
rate they endured his company in the hopes of an orange
shell. . . .

As soon as he reached the beach, Adela greeted him
excitedly.

"She's *here*," she said.

"Who?" said William blankly.

"Miss Twemlow," said Adela. "I've *seen* her. . . .
I've *spoken* to her. She's *staying* here. . . . I hope
Angela hasn't seen her. I shan't tell her she's here."

At this moment Angela came running down the slope
to the beach. She, too, looked flushed and excited. She
beckoned William to her and spoke in a mysterious
whisper.

"Don't tell Adela, but *she's* here. She's staying here. I've just spoken to her. Oh, William, she's more beautiful than ever."

"Where is she?" said William, interested despite himself.

"She's just going to her hotel at the end of the promenade. She's in a dark blue coat. You can't miss her. Do go and look at her, William. I can't tell you how beautiful she is. . . ."

William went up to the promenade and hurried to overtake the figure in the dark blue coat at the other end. He was vaguely gratified to find that Miss Twemlow was a very ordinary-looking woman, with short-sighted peering eyes, wearing a coat several inches longer than the fashionable length.

The next morning, however, the little girls' ardour was damped.

"Her fiancé's here," said Adela morosely. "At least he's not here, but he's staying five miles away, and he's going to come over by train every day. She won't come to tea with me. She won't even come for a walk. She says she would if her fiancé wasn't here. It's rotten luck, isn't it?"

"Well, I don't know . . ." said William.

"Of course it's rotten luck," said Adela hotly. "Suppose *your* favourite schoolmaster was here and you found that he couldn't come to tea because his fiancée was here, too, what would you feel like?"

"Gosh!" ejaculated William faintly, but before he could make any effort to describe his own attitude to his instructors, she went on:

"Anyway, she's coming to the Conservative Fête tomorrow. Perhaps he won't come to that. I do hope he doesn't come. I'm almost certain to get the wild flowers

prize. I did last year. And I'd love her to see me getting
it. . . ."

"What wild flowers prize?" said William.

"I'm a Junior Conservative," said Adela importantly, "and there's a competition for arranging wild
flowers. And they give a prize from the platform. And if
she was there without her stupid old fiancé it would be
glorious. 'Cause she'd see my wild flowers and prize and
everything. And I'd ask her to have tea with me. And
she would if *he* wasn't there. . . . I say, do go and find out
from that awful Angela if she's had the cheek to ask her
to tea."

William made his way across the beach to Angela,
who was kicking the sand about in a disconsolate
fashion.

"He's here," she greeted William. "I shan't get a
chance of seeing her with *him* here. He's coming over by
train every day. She won't even come to tea. . . . And I
was so excited when I heard she was coming to the
Conservative Fête to-morrow, but she says *he's* coming
too, so that means she won't have a minute for anything
else."

"Are you going in for that wild flower thing?" asked
William.

"Good gracious, no!" said Angela with fierce contempt. "I leave that rubbish to that awful Adela. But my
cousin's going to open the Fête. At least he's a sort of
cousin. His father's a cabinet minister and *he* was going
to come but he can't, so his son's coming. He's a second
or third cousin or something like that. But I've met him,
and I'd be able to introduce him to Miss Twemlow and
he'd have an ice cream or something with us. I know he
would. But, of course, if her fiancé's there, too, it
wouldn't be any fun. She doesn't take any interest in

anything when her fiancé's there. Oh, I wish I could *stop* him coming."

She was a much more attractive little girl than Adela. For one thing she was dark, and William had never preferred blondes. For another she had a wistful, drooping mouth, whereas Adela's was firm and somewhat aggressive.

"I'll stop him coming for you, if you like," said William.

The statement astonished him as much as it did Angela. He didn't know he was going to say it till he'd actually heard himself saying it.

She stared at him.

"You couldn't," she said.

William gave a slightly uneasy laugh.

"Oh yes, I could," he said, sticking to his guns. "Wouldn't be anythin' to me, that wouldn't."

"But *how* could you?" she persisted.

"Oh, I've got ways," he said mysteriously. "I've got ways, all right."

"But what ways?"

"I—I can't tell you," hedged William, "but I've gottem. I've got a—sort of *power* over people."

Her incredulity was fading into puzzled admiration.

"Oh, William," she said, "have you? Why didn't you tell me before?"

"There were reasons," said William. "I—well, I don't like people to know about this power I've got."

"I suppose they'd always be wanting you to do things?" said Angela.

"Yes," said William, thankfully accepting the explanation, "they'd always be wanting me to do things. But I'll do this for you, all right. I don't mind doin' this for you."

Angela's dark eyes shone with gratitude, and William preened himself in it, putting off the evil hour when he must make good his rash undertaking.

"It's wonderful of you," she was saying, and added, "if you really can."

"Oh, I can, all right," said William.

"He's coming by the 2.15 train," said Angela. Sudden anxiety clouded the eagerness of her dark eyes. "You won't—wreck the train, will you, William?"

"N-no," promised William, as if somewhat reluctantly. "No, if you don't want me to do that, I won't."

"I don't want anyone killed."

"All right," conceded William generously. "All right, I won't kill anyone."

"I jus' want him kept away. Quite kindly, I mean."

"I'll be as kind as I can," said William darkly. "One's gotter be a *bit* rough, doin' things like that. I always do 'em as kindly as I can."

"Oh, *William*!" said Angela. "Have you often kidnapped people?"

The awestruck admiration in her dark eyes went to William's head. He looked round in an exaggeratedly furtive manner.

"I'd better not tell you the things I've done," he said in a hoarse whisper. "I've done some things that—well, I'd jus' better not tell you 'em, that's all."

"You mean—you mean—the sort of things you read about in the newspaper?" said Angela breathlessly.

"Yes," said William, glad to have the details of his supposed crimes left to the imagination. "Yes, the sort you read in the papers."

The little girl heaved a deep sigh of mingled relief and ecstasy.

"I shan't worry a *bit* now," she said. "I *know* he

won't be there and that I shall have a lovely time with Miss Twemlow and my cousin. That awful Adela'll be *mad*. She doesn't know my cousin, and I shan't introduce her."

It didn't occur to William till he was on his way to the station the next afternoon that he had never seen Miss Twemlow's fiancé and so would not be able to recognise him when he arrived. But the reflection did not worry him for long. There probably wouldn't be many young men and he'd ask them all. Angela's admiration had made him look on himself as a superman. . . . A little obstacle like that was nothing to him. When the train steamed in he was relieved to see that only one young man descended from it. He was an amiable-looking young man with a slightly receding chin, slightly protruding eyes and a vague but eminently friendly smile. After one glance at him, William felt convinced that he couldn't be anyone but Miss Twemlow's fiancé. He had decided, however, that it might arouse his suspicions to ask him straight out if he were Miss Twemlow's fiancé. He had evolved a more subtle method of approach. He went up to the young man and, assuming a stern businesslike expression, said:

"'Scuse me. Are you goin' to the 'servative Fête?"

The young man brightened. He suggested a lost dog who has suddenly sighted its owner.

"Yes," he said. "Yes, that's where I'm bound, my young friend."

"Well, they sent me to show you the way," said William.

The young man's smile became brighter still.

"Jolly good of them!" he said. "Jolly good of them! Well, shall we start wending? The sooner it's over, the sooner to sleep, what?"

William found this calm unquestioning acceptance of the situation a little disconcerting. He had expected to have to use finesse, but apparently no finesse was demanded of him. He felt even a little disappointed. It was turning out almost too simple. . . .

"All right," he said. "Come on."

He was relieved to find that Miss Twemlow's fiancé did not know where the fête was to be held and that his carefully prepared and somewhat involved explanation—that the ground had been flooded during the night and the site had had to be changed—would not be necessary. (In view of the fact that it had not rained during the night he had felt that it might be difficult to sustain.) He steered Miss Twemlow's fiancé into a road that led in the opposite direction to that of the fête. Miss Twemlow's fiancé quite happily allowed himself to be steered.

"Hope I'm not late," he said.

"Oh, no," said William, "you're not late."

"Not too fond of these things, don't you know," Miss Twemlow's fiancé confessed, "but needs must when the devil drives, what?"

"Yes," said William, supposing that he meant Miss Twemlow by the devil.

When they had been walking for some time, William considered his next step. Miss Twemlow's fiancé was so far unsuspicious, but if they went on walking indefinitely his suspicions were bound to be aroused sooner or later. He had in fact already said, "About five minutes' walk from the station, isn't it?" and they had now been walking for at least ten.

"Nearly there, I suppose, aren't we, what?" he said suddenly, and William realised that something must be done at once or even this very trusting and gullible young

man might begin to smell a rat. They turned a bend in the
road, and there on a large open space by the roadside a
Fair was in progress. Merry-go-rounds went merrily
round, swings swung to dizzy heights, showmen shouted
and music blared. William clutched at the straw.

"Here we are," he said. "Here's the fête. . . ."

He looked at the young man apprehensively, but his
credulity was evidently still unstrained.

"Good!" he said. "Quite a jolly walk! But now to
business, what?" and turned in at the entrance of the
Fair. Inside, he stood and looked round with evident
approval.

"I say, this is jolly. No starch about this, what? Sort of
thing I like, don't you. Can't stand starch, what?"

William heaved a sigh of relief and entered the Fair
ground with his companion. His companion's approval
increased as they wandered round the booths and
swings.

"Jolly well arranged," he said. "No one fussing you
all the time. Hate being fussed, what?"

He looked about him as he walked. Looking for Miss
Twemlow, probably, thought William.

"Miss Twemlow said she might be late," he said,
taking the bull by the horns.

"That's a pity," said the young man vaguely, "but I
suppose it can't be helped, what?"

He didn't seem very sorry that Miss Twemlow might
be late, and, remembering Miss Twemlow, William
couldn't feel surprised by this.

They had reached a small platform upon which
normally a Strong Man challenged passers-by to a
boxing bout. The Strong Man, however, had vanished at
the moment in search of a quick one, and the Strong
Man's wife, resplendent in purple dress and plentifully

be-feathered hat, sat on the platform fanning herself with her hand.

"I suppose that's Lady Cynthia," said Miss Twemlow's fiancé uncertainly. "Never met any of them before, you know. Bit awkward in its way. Still, England expects, what?"

With an expansive smile he approached the feathered lady and wrung her hand.

"How d'you do, Lady Cynthia," he said. "So glad to see you. Hope I'm not late."

The feathered lady gave a scream of delight and swung his hand up and down.

"How d'you do, Sir Harchibald," she replied. "*Sow* good of you to come!"

"Not at all," deprecated Miss Twemlow's fiancé. "Only too glad. Well, shall we get on with the good work, what?"

He leapt upon the platform and began in a high-pitched nervous voice, "Ladies and gentlemen . . ."

The small crowd that had gathered to witness his greeting of the Strong Man's wife cheered, and others joined the crowd.

"I'm afraid I'm not much of a speaker," said Miss Twemlow's fiancé, "but I'll do my best."

Loud cheers greeted this. The orator looked gratified and continued:

"Well, I'm sure you don't want to waste any more time listening to me (Louder cheers) so I'll just declare this Sale of Work open and hope you'll all have a thoroughly enjoyable afternoon. Empty your purses and the stalls, what? On with the dance, let joy be unconfined, don't you know. And never forget that it's the Conservative party that made jolly old England what it is."

Wild applause broke out on all sides, and, blushing with pleasure, the orator leapt down from the platform, shook hands with the feathered lady, who was rocking with mirth, then set off through the crowd with William.

"That went off all right, don't you think?" he said complacently. "A jolly good audience, what? Mind you, I'm not a speaker. When I have to speak, my motto is 'Short and to the point.' That went down quite well, didn't it? Jolly old bird, Lady Cynthia. I always find those *nouveaux riches* easy to get on with. No starch, what? The old bird got my name wrong, but I can never remember names myself. Always dropping bricks with people's names."

The report that a new humorist had arrived on the scene spread far and wide, and a crowd was now accompanying them round the Fair. William, too, had enjoyed the joke. Everything in fact seemed to be going swimmingly.

"Got to do our duty and buy something, I suppose," Miss Twemlow's fiancé was saying. "Not so many of these so-called fancy stalls as usual, what? An improvement on the usual thing all round. Never been to one with less starch. Jolly good idea, what?"

He paused at the next stall and watched a man who was demonstrating pull-out toffee, pulling it out to the length of his arm like elastic and clapping it together again. Miss Twemlow's fiancé bought two pounds of it, which the man wrapped in a brown paper parcel. He then wandered on to a hoop-là stall, where, more by good luck than good management, he won an enormous vase of hideous design. Most of the crowd, disappointed by his failure to live up to his reputation as a humorist, had left him, but a small remnant was still faithful, and loudly cheered his winning of the vase. Miss Twemlow's fiancé was obviously enjoying himself. He continued to comment expansively on the unexpected absence of "starch".

"No idea it would be like this," he said. "Thought I'd have to pace round with a lot of bally old dowagers, buying tea cosies and saying polite what-nots. Always stumps me, that. Never know what to say to people. This is a reform, my young friend, that's long overdue, and I congratulate your little community down here on having thought of it. No doubt it will spread to other places like wild fire. Ye gods! When I think of the torment I've endured with dowagers, polite converse and tea cosies. . . . Come on, let's have a shy at a coconut."

Miss Twemlow's fiancé had an unexpectedly determined nature and, after the expenditure of one and sixpence in balls, succeeded in winning a coconut. He paid for William to try, but William was preoccupied and did himself less than justice. The situation could not, of course, be expected to continue at this stage indefinitely. Sooner or later the suspicions of the young man were bound to be aroused. Already he was evidently wondering in what capacity William had constituted himself his faithful bodyguard.

"I suppose you're Lady Cynthia's son, what?" he said carelessly.

"Gosh, no!" said William, then realised too late that it would have been safer to say "yes".

"Official of the Junior Branch, then, I suppose," said Miss Twemlow's fiancé, beaming at him. "Like the way they bring that to the fore these days. Youth at the helm, what? Perhaps that's why starch is on the wane. What about a ride on the gee-gees?"

William agreed. The church clock struck four. Well, at any rate, he thought, Adela and Angela would have had a clear hour with Miss Twemlow while he kept her fiancé at bay. Adela would have got the wild flowers prize, Angela would have introduced her to her cousin and he would have had an ice with them. They ought to be jolly grateful to him. He was getting a little tired of Miss Twemlow's fiancé, however, and thought he'd take him back to the station now as soon as possible. He must find some excuse, of course, for Miss Twemlow's non-appearance. Miss Twemlow's fiancé was climbing down from his wooden steed.

"Years since I went on a merry-go-round," he was saying happily. "What about a glass of lemonade?" They each drank a glass of synthetic liquid of a rich golden colour, which Miss Twemlow's fiancé pronounced excellent. Then William said:

"Well, I s'pose it's time you went back."

Miss Twemlow's fiancé looked at his watch.

"By Jove, I suppose it is," he said. "I'd better go and find Lady Cynthia."

"No, I wouldn't do that," said William. "I wouldn't do that. Well, she told me to tell you that she was busy an' she sent a message to say good-bye."

"Oh, that's all right," said Miss Twemlow's fiancé, relieved. "Decent old dame, but all this social stuff gets on one's nerves. That's what I've enjoyed about this afternoon. No—no——" He searched for a word.

"Starch," supplied William.

"That's it, by Jove!" said the young man, delighted. "No starch."

"Well, we'd better be gettin' to the station now," said William. "I don't think Miss Twemlow's goin' to be here. She said she might not."

"Yes, sorry not to have met Miss Twemlow," said the young man vaguely.

"She sent you love and kisses," said William.

"Very kind of her," said the young man, slightly taken aback. "Very kind indeed."

They were now on their way to the station, and William was congratulating himself on the final success of his scheme, when an old lady appeared round the bend of the road. William recognised her as an old lady staying at his hotel but hoped himself to escape recognition, as she was not one of those many inmates of the hotel who had objected to his various activities, and with luck might not even have noticed him. He was walking past her with a blank expressionless face when she stopped and said:

"Why, it's William! I should have thought you'd have been at the fête, dear."

"We've been there," said William.

"Yes, by Jove!" put in Miss Twemlow's fiancé, pointing in the direction of the Fair. "We've just come from it."

"I'm afraid you're mistaken," said the old lady. "The fête is in Sir Gerard Bannister's grounds about a quarter of a mile from here."

"By Jove!" said Miss Twemlow's fiancé. "You're joking!"

"I never joke," said the old lady. "I've just come from the fête myself! Good-day."

She walked on. They stood staring after her.

"I say!" said Miss Twemlow's fiancé. "We can't have made a mistake, can we?"

"No," said William desperately. "She's batty. I know her. She's stayin' at our hotel. She's batty. They let her go about alone 'cause she's not dangerous. She's jus' batty. She tells people things are in places where they aren't, like what she did now. No one takes any notice of her. Don't you worry about her. You go on home same as you were goin' to.'"

But Miss Twemlow's fiancé's conscience had evidently been roused. His bright all-embracing smile had faded. He looked worried.

"Think I'd better make sure," he said anxiously. "Don't want to make a hash of things. Promised the old man I'd do it in style, what?"

"But I tell you she doesn't know what she's talkin' about," pleaded William. "No one ever takes any notice of what she says. She's all right 'cept about places. She doesn't know where they are. She says they're in places where they aren't, same as she did jus' now. She——"

A look of calm determination had come into the young man's face.

"Tell you what I'll do," he said. "It's quite early, so I'll just walk along a bit and make sure. The old man said I'd probably make a hash of things, and I don't want the old bean to be able to say, 'I told you so.' Must go home with a clean escutcheon, what? Nice little walk for us both, and we'll feel then that we've left no stone unturned, no avenue unexplored, as the poet saith."

"All right," said William, yielding to the inevitable.

After all, he told himself, it didn't really matter. It was nearly five o'clock. Adela and Angela would have had all the afternoon with Miss Twemlow. Again he thought complacently of their gratitude and admiration. He had indeed gloriously vindicated his "power over people".

The next bend in the road brought them to the main gate of Sir Gerard Bannister's park and showed them the Conservative Fête in full swing. Posters advertised it. Loud speakers announced it. At that moment a military band struck up. The young man's mouth fell open.

"By Jove!" he said.

He looked round for William, but William was no longer to be seen. He was making his way through a small unauthorised opening in the palings into the park. He wanted to find Adela and Angela and receive their glowing thanks. He found Adela first. She was standing by herself, morosely watching a putting competition.

"Well," William greeted her complacently, "I kept him away all right, didn't I?"

She stared at him.

"Kept who away?" she demanded.

"Miss Twemlow's what-d'you-call-it," said William. "I kept him away, all right, didn't I?"

Her small face stiffened with anger.

"D'you think you're funny?" she asked in withering contempt.

It was William's turn to stare at her.

"Well, didn't I keep him away?" he challenged.

"Keep him away!" she echoed furiously. "He's been here all afternoon."

"He—but he couldn't have been," said the bewildered William. "I've been with him. I've kept him away. . . . I've kept him away so's you would get your wild flowers prize an'——"

"Wild flowers prize!" she repeated. "They didn't even judge them, and *she* wouldn't have seen if I *had* got it 'cause *he* was there all the time."

The world seemed to spin round William.

"He—Why didn't they judge them?"

"'Cause the man who was going to open the fête and judge the wild flowers never turned up," said Adela venomously. "Never turned up. And they were all so worried what had happened to him that they didn't even get anyone else to do it. They said that we could have it again at one of the ordinary meetings. As if that's any good to me! I wanted *her* to see me get the prize, and she was talking to *him* all the time. I shouldn't have minded that so much if I'd got the prize. I could have showed it her, anyway. She'd have had to have *looked* at it and known I'd won it, but with that man that was going to judge them not turning up——"

"But look here," interrupted William. "He *can't* have been here. Miss Twemlow's what-d'you-call-it, I mean. He was with me all the time." He looked round. "Where is he? Show me him."

"He's gone," said Adela. "They've both gone. They went about five minutes ago."

"What was he like?" said William.

Adela stamped angrily.

"I'm sick of answering silly questions. What does it matter what he was like? You said you'd keep him away and you didn't. I've had a *horrible* afternoon, and it's all your fault."

"But listen——" said William, "you must have made a mistake. You——"

Adela, however, refused to listen. She turned away from him impatiently and disappeared in the crowd.

Bewildered and apprehensive, William wandered off. Almost at once he came upon Angela. She was watching Bowling for a Live Pig with an air of suffering patience.

He accosted her cautiously:

"I say," he said, "I *did* stop him. I did, honest. I met him at the station an'——"

She swung round on him.

"You story teller!" she said. "He's been here all the time. . . . You're just a *story* teller, that's what you are. Making out you can do things, an' all the time you can't."

"I'm not. I'm not, honest," pleaded William. "I did keep him away. Listen, I——"

"I've had a *miserable* afternoon," went on Angela. "My cousin didn't come at all. He was supposed to be opening it, but he never came at all. I shouldn't have minded *him* being here so much if my cousin had come, too. I could have introduced her to him, anyway, and he'd have given us an ice and that would have been better than *nothing*."

A horrible suspicion was taking form in William's mind. He looked about him. Standing near was a group of fashionably-dressed and worried-looking women, talking in agitated but lowered voices. He drew near to listen.

"But, my dear," one of them was saying, "I can't *think* what's happened. They say he caught the train at the other end. There's no doubt of that. And we've rung up the police and there haven't been any accidents. What on *earth* can have happened to him?"

At that moment William's companion of the afternoon could be seen making his way towards them. He still wore his radiant and all-embracing smile. He still carried his vase, his two coconuts and his parcel of pull-out toffee.

"I say," he said, "I'm so terribly sorry. I've only just realised. I went to the wrong place. The boy——" His eye fell on William and his smile grew yet more radiant and all-embracing as he recognised him. "There he is! A jolly good little scout he is, too, but we went to the wrong show. He——"

It was at this point that William, throwing ceremony to the winds, turned and made good his escape.

*   *   *

**WILLIAM, THROWING CEREMONY TO THE WINDS, TURNED
AND MADE GOOD HIS ESCAPE.**

It was the next morning. William walked jauntily
along the promenade. He'd got up before breakfast and
gone down to the beach and found two orange shells.
Two orange shells. . . . One, of course, would have
caused a certain awkwardness, but two! . . . He'd made
a little mistake yesterday (how could he have known that

"I'M SO TERRIBLY SORRY. I'VE ONLY JUST REALISED.
I WENT TO THE WRONG PLACE," SAID WILLIAM'S COMPANION.

Miss Twemlow's fiancé was going to change his mind
and come by car?) but the orange shells would put things
right. Adela and Angela would be so grateful for the
orange shells that they'd forget all about yesterday.
He'd be a hero, a superman—a boy who could find two
orange shells in five minutes when they'd been looking

for them in vain for weeks. He hoped it would make them friends again. He wanted to make them friends before he went home. He'd got a piece of good news for them, too. Someone staying at the hotel knew Miss Twemlow and said that her fiancé had to go to London on business for the next two days. She'd be able to go for walks with Adela and Angela now and have tea with them. They'd be jolly grateful to him for finding that out. . . .

He had felt a bit apprehensive after his mistake of yesterday but nothing had happened. The young man had so evidently enjoyed his visit to the Fair, and his account of the part William had played in the matter was so confused, that the authorities had decided to take no steps. He had probably asked the boy the way, they decided, and the boy, himself a stranger to the district, had thought he meant the Fair. . . . Not knowing William, they gave him the benefit of the doubt—a benefit that was seldom accorded to him in his home surroundings. He had spent an anxious evening, but no irate Conservative arrived at the hotel to lay the case before his father, and this morning the danger of that was safely over. And he'd found two orange shells and had discovered that Miss Twemlow's fiancé was going away. . . .

Suddenly he saw them coming along the promenade together. They were walking arm-in-arm. Obviously they had made friends. That was a good thing. They'd be easier to get on with together than several yards apart. He approached them with a triumphant smile and held out his palm, on which reposed the two orange shells.

"Look!" he said in serene confidence of their gratitude and delight.

They stared blankly, first at the shells and then at William.

"Well?" said Adela coldly.

"I—I—well, you *wanted* an orange shell, didn't you?" said William, taken aback.

The scene wasn't going at all as he'd imagined it going. He couldn't understand it. . . . Where were the cries of delight, the "Oh, William, *thank* you. How clever of you."

"Good gracious!" said Angela with an affected laugh. "Fancy you remembering that! We did play with shells once, I remember, when we'd nothing else to do, but we found it very babyish and boring, didn't we, Adela?"

"My goodness, yes!" shrilled Adela. "Can't think what anyone *sees* in the things."

"Fancy a great boy like you wasting your time over them!" said Angela, looking with dramatic contempt from the shells in William's outstretched hand to William himself.

The world rocked round him.

"But listen," he pleaded. "Listen. He's goin' away— the what-d'you-call-it. She can come out to tea with you to-day an' to-morrow."

Adela's wide-open eyes registered amused bewilderment.

"Who on earth are you talking about?"

"Miss Twemlow," said William.

Two heads were tossed disdainfully, two peals of scornful laughter rang out.

"My *goodness*!" said Adela. "*That* woman!"

"As if," said Angela, "we ever wanted to see her again!"

"*Or* you," said Adela. "Come on, Angela, darling! Don't let's waste any more time."

They walked on. William stared after them open-mouthed. At the end of the short promenade they swung round and walked back. They still walked arm-in-arm, heads close together, talking in confidential undertones. As they passed William they lifted their noses in aloof disgust, but this time did not even look at him. . . .

Chapter 5

William and the Air Raid Shelter

William and Ginger trudged away from the Hall dispiritedly. Just before the war Mrs. Bott had had a new artificial lake made in the grounds, and the Outlaws had adopted it as one of their favourite haunts. But the war had got on Mrs. Bott's nerves, and she had that morning forbidden them to go near it again. She had complained about her gas mask (she said that it suffocated her) and been snubbed by her air raid warden (who didn't seem to think it mattered whether she was suffocated or not), and so it was perhaps natural that she should, in her turn, take it out of the Outlaws. In any case she hadn't liked William's manner when he was acting as messenger in the sub-report centre and she was at the telephone. It was the first time she had had to use the telephone there (she was, as she put it, "all of a fluster"), and he had informed her with, she thought, undue politeness that she was dialling the number without removing the receiver. . . .

"I don't want you messin' about any more," she had said. "Sick and tired of you, that's what I am. Corst a pot of money, this lake did, an' I didn't make it to have boys muckin' about in it."

Mrs. Bott on occasions could display an almost over-powering amount of refinement, but in moments of irritation it was apt to desert her.

"What *did* you make it for, then?" asked William.

"I made it for the voo, of course," snapped Mrs. Bott. "What else are lakes for? Not for boys muckin' about in 'em, I can tell you *that*. Bad enough with all these excavated kids about, without you startin' muckin' about."

Mrs. Bott's command over the King's English was a precarious one, and the word "evacuated" had always eluded her.

"A' right," muttered William. "A'right. A'right. It's a rotten ole pond, anyway."

Mrs. Bott's fat little face turned from pink to purple. She quivered with jelly-like rage.

"Rotten indeed!" she spluttered. "Pond indeed! D'you know how much the hartificial lake cost, you little monkey? More than your father makes in a dozen years, I'll be bound."

"My father's a millionaire," said William calmly. "He pretends not to be jus' for fun, but he is one, all right. He—he could buy Buckingham Palace if he wanted to, but he doesn't want to. He doesn't like it. He could make a dozen lakes if he wanted to, but he doesn't like lakes. He thinks they're silly. He's thinkin' of havin' a nartificial sea made one day. He——"

"Get off with you!" said Mrs. Bott angrily.

"A'right," said William loftily. "I'm jus' gettin' off," and added meaningly: "You'll be jolly sorry for this one day."

He stopped to collect his boats from the pond, then walked away with slow dignity, accompanied by Ginger. They turned when they reached the drive to see the fat fur-clad figure of Mrs. Bott waddling away in the distance towards the house.

"She's an ole toad, that's what she is," said William. "An ole *toad*."

"Why did you say she'd be sorry one day?" asked Ginger.

"Well, she will," said William vaguely. "When I'm grown up and Prime Minister or somethin' like that, I bet she'll be jolly sorry. There's things I could do," darkly, "when I'm Prime Minister that'd make her jolly sorry she turned me off her ole pond."

"How d'you know you're goin' to be Prime Minister?" said Ginger.

"Well," admitted William, "I might be the head of Scotland Yard. I've not quite made up my mind, but I'm goin' to be somethin' important, whatever I am."

"You said yesterday you were goin' to be a man what drives a steam roller," Ginger reminded him.

"I can do that, anyway," said William. "I bet a Prime Minister or the head of Scotland Yard can drive a steam roller, can't they? It'd be a nice change from a motor car, an' people'd have to get out of the way. . . . Serve her jolly well right if I ran over her in my steam roller. I bet when you're Prime Minister you can run over who you like. . . ."

"What're we goin' to do now we can't play submarines on her lake?" demanded Ginger.

William considered. The war had distinctly curtailed their activities. Farmers, laying out more land for vegetable growing, were impatient of trespassers. Land army girls, imported from towns, showed scant sympathy with William and his concerns.

"I can't be bothered with you," was the response of all grown-ups to their claims. "There's a war on . . ."

"Tell you what," he said as a sudden idea struck him. "Let's go'n' play submarines in her dugout."

"Whose?"

"Mrs. Bott's."

Ginger gasped.

"We daren't," he said. "She'd be *mad*."

"She won't know," said William. "She's scared stiff of it. I heard my mother say so. She never goes in, even if there's a raid warning. . . . An' it's a jolly fine one. . . . We can pretend it's a submarine. . . . Come on."

"She'll see us . . ." protested Ginger.

"No, she won't," said William. "I know a way of gettin' to it through the shrubbery. They've made a sort of rock'ry round it. It's jolly fine. . . . Come on."

Ginger hesitated. He wasn't really anxious for another encounter with Mrs. Bott, but there didn't seem anything else to do, and one must do something. . . .

"A'right," he said. "But she'll be *mad* if she finds us."

"Huh! I'm not frightened of ole Mrs. Toad," said William with a swagger.

He led the way on all fours through a shrubbery, on the outskirts of which a brand new rockery concealed the entrance to the Botts' dugout. Ginger followed him down a flight of steps between high concrete walls to a stout green-painted door.

"They don't keep it locked," whispered William. "I've explored here before."

He pulled open the door, and they entered a cheerful little compartment, with yellow walls, arm chairs, electric kettle, wash basin, embroidered face towels, and two bunks against the wall, furnished with rugs and lilos.

"They can sleep here," said William, almost with the pride of proprietorship. "See? One on each shelf. Bet.

they look funny, don't you? An' have tea an' all. There's tinned things in that meat safe. An' these little holes," he pointed to two small pipes protruding from the walls at either end, "are to let in air, an' when there's gas they can screw tops on to 'em to keep it out. Gosh! I wouldn't like to be Hitler after these two. He'll *never* get 'em. His only chance is her bein' too scared to come in. . . . I say, it makes a jolly fine submarine, doesn't it? I'll be captain first, shall I? There's an enemy coming. Get a torpedo. Bang! Bang. . . . *Got* it! Now, dive quick."

At the end of half an hour's strenuous naval activity Ginger suddenly said:

"Crumbs! It's nearly tea time. An' that girl's comin' to tea."

"What girl?" said William.

"That girl what's come to stay with Mrs. Monks," said Ginger. "She was in England when the war broke out, an' she's not been able to go back. She's an Icelander."

"Gosh!" said William. "Is she all dressed in furs?"

"Dunno. I've not seen her yet."

"'Spect she lives in a snow house at home."

"'Spect she does," agreed Ginger.

"An' eats dried fish an' drives about on sledges with reindeer."

"'Spect so," said Ginger.

"They don't wash at all in winter," said William enviously. "I bet she's jolly dirty. Gosh! I wish I lived there. Can I come and have a look at her?"

"Yes," said Ginger, and added, "I don't think we've got any dried fish for tea."

"That's all they eat," said William firmly, "an' they eat it with their fingers, an' they dress in furs all over, feet an' all, an' never wash. Crumbs! It must be fun."

It was a distinct disappointment, therefore, to be introduced to a little girl with dark curls and large solemn blue eyes, daintily dressed in white socks and a rose-coloured woollen frock. William stared at her.

"Where's your furs?" he demanded.

The little girl shook her head.

"I—do—not—understand—English—very—well," she said slowly and carefully. ·

"Furs," said Ginger, making a large indeterminate gesture, as if to explain his meaning. "Furs off animals." He made another sweeping gesture meant to indicate animals.

The little girl shook her head.

"I—do—not—understand," she said.

"Look!" said William, pointing from the fur rug on the hearth to the little girl's dress, "wear that at home, don't you?"

The little girl shook her head.

"I—wear—the—dress—I—wear—now."

They stared at her blankly.

"But you live in a snow house, don't you?" said Ginger almost pleadingly.

"Snow house?" said the little girl.

"What sort of house do you live in at home?" said William slowly.

"A—house—like—this," said the little girl.

"Gosh!" said William. "Fancy buildin' a house like this on all those miles an' miles of snow an' ice."

She stared at him uncomprehendingly.

They inspected her in silence.

"She looks jolly clean," said William at last with frowning disapproval.

"P'raps they've washed her since she came to England," suggested Ginger.

"Yes, I bet that's it," said William. "I bet she came over all dirty an' dressed in furs. I bet she lives in a snow house. She was jus' puttin' on side pretendin' she didn't."

He turned to the little girl, who was still staring at him solemnly.

"You *do* drive about with reindeers, anyway," he said, fixing her with a stern eye. "I bet you drive about with reindeers, at home. When you come out of your snow houses at the end of the winter, I mean," he said.

"I—do—not—understand," said the little girl.

"What—do—you—drive—in—at—home?" said William patiently.

"Oh yes, I understand," said the little girl. "A motor car."

"*Gosh!*" said William in disgust. "I *bet* she's puttin' it all on! I *bet* she lives in a snow house an' doesn't wash an' eats dried fish. Stands to reason she does in a country like that."

But Ginger's mother, entering the room at that moment, put the final touch to their disillusionment.

"You're thinking of Lapland, you little idiots," she said. "Solrun comes from a town called Reykjavik which is like any town in England. There are motor cars and taxis and hotels and shops."

"Doesn't she live in a snow house an' not wash and eat dried fish, then?" demanded Ginger.

"Of course not," said Ginger's mother. "What an idea! . . . She's very homesick and I want you two boys to play with her and cheer her up."

"Play with her!" echoed Ginger in disgust. "Us play with a kid like that!"

But there was the ghost of a dimple in the little girl's

cheek, and neither Ginger nor William was proof against a dimple.

"We've other things to do than play with a kid like *that*," said William with a ferocity that was meant to conceal his weakening.

"Let's take her to see our submarine," whispered Ginger, and William realised with relief that Ginger was weakening, too.

"She'd only tell people about it an' we'd get into a row," said William scornfully. "A kid like that always *tells*."

"You *bet*!" agreed Ginger. "A *girl*, too. They're always the worst."

Having thus affirmed their superiority, they felt at liberty to play Ludo with the little girl. She didn't cheat and was a good loser, but she remained sad and wistful-looking. The dimple peeped out faintly and only at rare intervals.

"She's so homesick it's making her quite ill," William heard Mrs. Monks say to Ginger's mother. "Her aunt sent her to me to see if I could cheer her up, but I can't do anything. Her people don't think it's safe for her to be sent back just yet, but she's simply pining away."

That evening William approached Mr. Brown just as he was settling down to his evening paper.

"Do you know anything about Iceland, Father?" he said.

Mr. Brown looked up at him coldly.

"*Need* you eat nuts all over me?" he enquired.

"No," said William patiently, retreating a few feet. "I'm not eatin' 'em over you now. Do you know anything about Iceland?"

"Don't talk with your mouth full," said Mr. Brown, returning to his paper.

William, seeing that his parent was in what his family called his Special Constable mood, swallowed a mouthful of half-masticated nuts before he spoke again.

"I've finished 'em now, Father," he gulped. "Do you know anythin' about Iceland?"

It happened that Mr. Brown had recently read an article on Iceland in a monthly journal and was, therefore, torn between a natural desire to repress his irrepressible younger son and an equally natural desire to display his knowledge.

"How long is it since you washed your face?" he demanded. "Its chief characteristic is its hot springs."

"I'm *always* washin' it," said William pathetically. "I've gotter sort of *dark* skin, that's why it looks dirty." He slipped another nut into his mouth and went on: "What sort of hot springs?"

"Just hot springs," said Mr. Brown. "Hot water coming up out of the earth. . . . Do you *ever* stop eating?"

"I only eat when I'm hungry," explained William. "I'm nearly always hungry, that's why I'm nearly always eating. How d'you mean, hot water coming out of the earth? Hot water *can't* come out of the earth."

"It can in Iceland," said Mr. Brown. "It comes out boiling in a sort of fountain. It's called a geyser."

"Thought a geyser was a thing in a bathroom," said William.

"You thought wrong, then," said Mr. Brown, taking up his paper with an air of finality.

William stood digesting this information in silence for a few moments.

"Hot springs?" he said at last incredulously. "But—listen. Water can't be hot if you don't boil it. You can't *boil* it down in the earth."

Mr. Brown continued to read his newspaper without answering.

"Listen!" said William again, as vehemently as if his father had entered into a heated argument with him. "*Listen!* Water's not hot natural. Water's cold natural. You've gotter boil it to make it hot. Same as a kitchen boiler or—or—or a gas ring or somethin'. Stands to reason water can't be hot nat'ral."

Mr. Brown continued to read his paper unmoved.

"Well, all I can say is it *can't*," said William. "The *ground's* cold, isn't it? Well, water can't come out of it hot, then, can it? If ground was hot, people couldn't walk on it. It'd burn their shoes up. Stands to reason, doesn't it?"

Mr. Brown turned over a page of his newspaper, absorbed in the leading article.

"Doesn't it?" repeated William, almost with pleading in his voice.

Mr. Brown glanced up at him.

"Your face is filthy," he said dispassionately, "your hair is like an unmown lawn, your stockings are coming down, and you are standing in my light."

"Huh!" ejaculated William, turning away with a gesture of disgust. "Huh! Cracked, that's what he is," he muttered when he had reached a safe distance. "Thinks ground's hot. Huh! That's jolly funny, that is. Thinks ground's hot. Thinks water comes out of it boiling. Gosh! He's cracked, all right."

He went to Ginger's house and found that Solrun had already arrived, having been sent by Mrs. Monks in the hope that the society of her contemporaries would dispel her homesickness. She looked more serious and wistful than ever. William decided to cheer her up.

"I've gotter jolly good joke," he said. "It'll make you

laugh all right. My father thought that water came out of the ground *hot* in Iceland. *Hot!* Fancy that. Cracked, that's what he is. Thought it came out of the ground in a sort of fountain. *Hot* water! I've been laughing ever since."

The little girl stared at him. Laboriously he explained the joke again.

"But it does," she said earnestly, when he had finished. "It *does* come out—hot. Like a beautiful— fountain, you call it. Just near where I live. Oh," her blue eyes suddenly swam with tears. "Oh, how I should love to see one of them again!"

Still trying to cheer her up, they took her through the woods and showed her their favourite haunts. She was politely interested but no more. The veil of impenetrable sadness still seemed to hang over her. A resolve was forming itself in William's mind. She *should* see one of them again. It would cheer her up no end. Just hot water. Easy enough to arrange. It would want a bit of thinking out, of course, but he'd think it out all right. He was jolly good at thinking things out. . . .

"We used to go down to the lake at the Hall every day," Ginger was saying. "It was jolly fine. We had submarines there. Then *she* came down and kicked up a fuss an' stopped us. We weren't doin' any harm at all, but she came along an' kicked up a fuss an' stopped us. We go in her ole dugout now an' pretend it's a submarine, but it's not as good. It's a secret, about her dugout. We don't want anyone to know . . ."

The little girl watched his face with earnest blue eyes as he talked, trying to follow his meaning. She nodded eagerly when she understood.

"It's a secret," repeated Ginger. "You won't tell anyone, will you?"

"No," promised the little girl. "I—will—not—tell."

"You can come to it this afternoon," said Ginger generously. "Can't she, William?"

"Yes," said William, "an' I've gotter s'prise for her. Something that'll cheer her up."

She looked at him questioningly.

"A s'prise for you," William informed her. "Somethin' you'll jolly well like."

The little girl looked mystified.

"Yes, please," she said politely.

* * *

As they approached the rockery William drew Ginger aside.

"You take her in an' show it her," he said. "I've gotter stay out here an' fix up that s'prise for her."

"What is it?" asked Ginger.

"You wait an' see," said William, mysteriously. "It's a jolly fine one."

"All right," said Ginger.

He led the little girl down into the dugout.

"We play that it's our submarine," he explained. "It's not so good as playin' by the lake, but she stopped us doin' that. Anyway, it's not bad. This is the captain's bunk, an' this is where we keep our torpedoes, an' this is——"

There came the sound of footsteps descending the steps.

"Crumbs!" gasped Ginger. "Someone's comin'. Hide, quick!"

He pulled her down into the corner between the meat safe and the wall. Almost immediately the door opened, and Mrs. Bott's plump fur-clad figure waddled into the room. Her face wore an expression of mingled pride and terror. Lady Markham from Upper Marleigh had asked to come and see her dugout, and Mrs. Bott had invited her to tea the next day. She was torn between her nervousness of the dugout and her desire to show it off adequately to her distinguished visitor. She had determined to come down alone and try to overcome her fear of it. She wanted, moreover, to rehearse the process of "showing off", so that it should lack nothing in impressiveness.

She stood just inside the doorway and looked around, an expression of ludicrous dismay on her pink fat face.

"Oh, crikey!" she moaned. "I know something'll 'appen. I told Botty so. *H*appen." (Whenever Mrs. Bott realised that she had dropped an aitch she always picked it up again, even if it was a little late.) "It ain't natural, diggin' down in the earth like rats. I keep thinkin' of that there lake. . . ." Then she remembered the object of her visit and assumed a bright set smile together with her most refined accent. "Come hin, Lady Markham," she said in a high-pitched, genteel voice. "'Ere's hour little dugout. Solid concrete walls, you see, an' all. Reinforced with metal an' painted a pleasing shade of yeller. Looks a treat, don't it?" Her face sagged again into dismay as she looked round. "Oh, lor! Oh, lor! I can't bear to think of sittin' 'ere 'our after 'our with them there aeroplanes messin' about over'ead. An' all very well Botty sayin' the lake couldn't come in. You can't never tell—not with water. *H*over *h*ead. Me an' Botty swimmin' round an' round here like a couple o' goldfish. Fair gives me the jimjams to think of it. Come to that, we can't swim, neither of us. Oh, crikey!" She remembered her imaginary visitor, and hastily resumed her set bright smile and refined accent. "I've forgot 'ow many tons of concrete was used in the construction of this 'ere shelter, but Botty could tell you. It'd fair take your breath away.

Electricity laid on an' all. 'And basins to wash our 'ands in and food in the meat safe. *H*ands."

Ginger shrank further into his corner and drew the little girl with him, but Mrs. Bott had already moved on.

"Of course, Botty an' me never touch tinned ordinary. Four course dinner, we 'ave every night. But then we've all got to make sacrifices in war time, 'aven't we? Look . . . electric kettle. Everything the 'eart could desire, as Botty puts it. Quite lit'ry, Botty is sometimes. *H*eart. An' here's the bunks where we can lay down nice as nip." Again her features sagged into comic dismay and her voice into its familiar cockney intonation. "Crikey! it won't be 'alf cheerful, layin' 'ere an' thinkin' wot's goin' to 'appen. Wish I felt surer of that there lake. Wish I 'adn't 'ad it done now. Never did trust water." She looked with distaste at the plump inflated lilo in the lower bunk. "Botty said I oughter try layin' on it jus' for practice. Well, I'd better, I suppose. Can't say I fancy it—— The best lilos money can buy, Lady Markham. Hever so comfy. Botty says we'll quite enjoy a hair raid on them, but, of course, that's only 'is wit. I'm on the lower one along of it bein' easier to get into. Botty's gotter little ladder to climb into his, made strong special to bear his weight. He's been practisin', an' he nips into it a fair treat now. . . . I'll lay down an' you can see 'ow comfy it looks. . . ."

Mrs. Bott scrambled laboriously on to the lower bunk and lay there for a moment or two with her eyes tightly screwed up. Then she opened them. . . . And at that precise moment William launched his "surprise". He had meant to reproduce a geyser in order to assuage the little girl's homesickness, but the scheme had been beset with difficulties. Hot water, of course, was easy enough to obtain, but it was less easy to stage a realistic fountain.

For a fountain, water had to go up and down. He could make it go down but he couldn't make it go up . . . and so he had finally decided that it was enough to make it go down. After all, in a fountain it was the going down water that one noticed. Probably she wouldn't even notice that it didn't go up-first. . . . The air pipe leading into Mrs. Bott's dugout had given him the idea of producing his geyser there while Ginger and the little girl were looking round inside. The kettle of boiling water that he had brought from home was no longer hot, but it was still fairly warm. He had found the carefully guarded outlet of the air pipe in the rockery, and had brought a small length of rubber tubing (fetched from Robert's motor cycle shed) to fit on to the end of it. Through this pipe he began to pour the contents of his kettle, fondly imagining the little girl clapping her hands in delight, as the "geyser" appeared. It was on to this sudden spurt of water that Mrs. Bott opened her eyes. She gave a loud scream, leapt with unexpected agility from her bunk, and rushed from the room. Ginger and Solrun came out of their hiding places. After a short interval William joined them. The scream had disconcerted him. It wasn't a thin little girl's scream of joyful surprise. It was a fat woman's scream of horror.

The little girl was in the middle of the room laughing helplessly.

"Oh, how—funnee—she—was!" she said. "How—funnee!"

They looked at her in surprise. It was the first time they had seen her laugh.

"What happened?" demanded William. "Who did that yell?"

"Ole Mrs. Bott was here," explained Ginger. "She did it."

"Crumbs!" said William aghast and, as the full horror of the situation dawned on him, "*Corks!*"

"It's all right. She didn't see us," explained Ginger. "We were hidin' behind the meat safe."

"WHAT HAPPENED?" DEMANDED WILLIAM. "WHO DID THAT YELL?"

"Did you like the geyser?" said William anxiously to the little girl.

The little girl was still laughing.

"Oh—it—was—so—funnee," she said.

"Well, it's cheered her up, all right," said William proudly.

Ginger was gazing with consternation at the swamped floor.

"Gosh! we'd better do somethin'," he said. "There'll

"OH, HOW—FUNNEE—SHE—WAS!" SAID SOLRUN. "HOW—FUNNEE!"

be an awful row if anyone sees it."

"A'right. We'll swash it up," said William carelessly.

He took up one of the towels from the towel rail, wiped up the water as best he could, flung the towel under the bed, then moved a rug from its position by the bunks to cover the damp patch on the floor. Fortunately, it was a small kettle, and he had spilt a good deal of it on the way. The geyser had been less prolific than he had meant it to be. . . .

"Come on, quick," said Ginger. "Let's get out. She'll come back in a minute and kick up an awful row."

*   *   *

Mrs. Bott had flung herself into the Library, where Mr. Bott was sitting at his desk, trying to think out a telling war-time slogan for Bott's sauce. He had just discarded "Bott's for Britons" in favour of "Win the war on Bott's".

He jumped up at sight of his wife.

"Whatever's the matter, Maria?" he said.

Mrs. Bott collapsed on to the sofa.

"Oh dear! Oh dear!" she wailed hysterically. "Oh dear! Oh dear! Oh dear! I told you it'd 'appen Botty. I told you an' you wouldn't listen. *H*appen."

Mr. Bott came across to the sofa and sat down by her, patting her hand reassuringly.

"Pull yourself together, Maria, and tell me what 'appened."

"*H*appened, Botty," Mrs. Bott corrected him between her gasps.

"All right," said Mr. Bott propitiatorily, "'appened, then. What is it?"

Mrs. Bott's emotion at the memory of what it was deepened.

"You can't never say I didn't warn you," she moaned. "Over and over again I did. I warned you and warned you. And now it's 'appened."

"But what?" demanded the mystified Mr. Bott. "What's 'app—what is it?"

"The lake's come in an' flooded the shelter," said Mrs. Bott dramatically. "Come in in great waves, it did. Right over my shoes. I only jus' got out in time. Jus' think, we might 'ave been in there when it 'appened, layin' in them bunks drowned dead. Oh, Botty!"

"There, there, Maria!" said Mr. Bott, patting her hand again. "Don't take on so."

"It give me such a *turn*," groaned Mrs. Bott. "I'll never forget it till my dyin' day. Wave on wave of it *pourin'* in. What it must be like now I can't a-bear to think. Up to the ceilin', I should think. Everythin' soaked—lilos an' all. It set my 'eart goin' like a dynamite. *H*eart."

"Dynamo, Maria," Mr. Bott corrected her mildly. "But—but where did this 'ere water come from?"

"From the lake, of course," said Mrs. Bott. "Oh, Botty, don't say I didn't warn you. Through the little air hole, it came. Wave on wave of it *pourin'* in. If I'd stayed a minute later I'd 've been drowned. It was very nearly up to my knees when I left."

"But look here, Maria," protested Mr. Bott. "It *couldn't* have come from the lake."

"I told you it would," moaned Mrs. Bott. "I *told* you. . . ."

"I know you did," said Mr. Bott, "and I told you it wouldn't. The architect an' the builder told you it couldn't."

"Jus' think if Vi'let Elizabeth 'ad been in," said Mrs. Bott, surrendering to a fresh wave of emotion. "*Oh!*"

"Well, she wasn't," said Mr. Bott. "She's safe at school. An', anyway, the lake couldn't have flowed into the shelter. It's against nature."

"Don't talk to me about nature," said Mrs. Bott darkly. "I've got eyes, 'aven't I? I can see when water comes pourin' into a place an' when it doesn't, can't I? If you don't believe me, come an' see for yourself."

"Yes, I'd like to," said Mr. Bott simply.

"Mind you," Mrs. Bott warned him, "it's fairly goin' into the jaws of danger. The water must be up to the ceiling now."

"I'll risk that," said Mr. Bott.

"*Pourin'* in, it was. Wave upon wave."

"Don't you come, then, dear."

"Yes, I'll come," said Mrs. Bott. "I'll come all right. If we've gotter be drowned, let's be drowned together."

"I don't think it'll come to that, love," Mr. Bott reassured her.

Outside the shelter he paused a moment, then flung open the door. The little room lay there empty and peaceful before them—the bunks, the meat safe, the electric fire, the hand basin. . . . Neither noticed that the towel had disappeared and that the mat was moved from its old position by the bunks to the other end of the room.

Mr. Bott turned to his wife.

"Well, Maria," he said in mild sarcasm, "where's all this water you was tellin' me about?"

Mrs. Bott was gazing round, her goggle-like eyes open wide in incredulous amazement.

"But—I *saw* it, Botty," she gasped. "I *saw* it as plain as plain. Pourin' through the air hole, it was. . . ."

"Well, where is it, that's what I'd like to know," said Mr. Bott.

She pointed to the bunk.

"I was layin' down there an——" She stopped short as an idea struck her. "P'raps I'd dropped off," she said. "P'raps it was a dream."

Mr. Bott smiled indulgently.

"That's more like it," he said. "It sounded like a dream to me all along."

Mrs. Bott sat down on the bunk and stared in front of her.

"But if it was a dream, Botty, it must *mean* something," she said slowly.

"Nonsense!" smiled Mr. Bott.

"But it *must*," said Mrs. Bott. "Botty," earnestly, "it's a *warning*, that's what it is. It was sent to warn us that the lake's *goin'* to flood it."

"I tell you it couldn't possibly, Maria."

She looked at him solemnly.

"Well, what was the dream sent me for, then?" she demanded.

He spread out his hands.

"Well—it was just an ordinary dream, like."

She shook her head.

"No, it wasn't, Botty," she said. "It was—it was that *vivid*. I've never 'ad a dream as vivid as what that one was. *Had.* Botty, if I'd not come down 'ere an' seen with me own eyes—I'd never 'ave believed. I tell you, I saw the waves pouring in. Well, it was that vivid, it was more a vision than a dream, as you might say. . . . Botty, it *must* mean somethin'."

"But what *could* it mean, Maria?" said Mr. Bott.

"I've told you, Botty. It means it's *goin'* to flood the place."

"Maria," said Mr. Bott patiently, "didn't you 'ear me say it *couldn't.*"

"How couldn't it?" Mrs. Bott challenged him. "The lake could overflow, like, an' come over the lawn an' the shrubbery an' pour down the 'ole same as it did in my dream. *H*ole."

"Well, someone would *see* it if it did."

"No one might be there to see," said Mrs. Bott. "It might 'appen sudden. *H*appen. . . . We can't very well keep someone down there watchin' all the time——" Her eyes opened wide and she drew in her breath as a sudden idea struck her. "Botty! Them boys!"

"What boys?" said the mystified Mr. Bott.

"Them boys!" repeated Mrs. Bott. "Quick, let's go 'n' see if we can find 'em."

She hurried out of the shelter and looked around her.

William and Ginger, who were interestedly watching events from the edge of the shrubbery, hastily dived into the undergrowth—just too late to avoid the roving eye of Mrs. Bott.

"Come 'ere, boys," she called, and added absently: "*H*ere."

As trespassers on her property their first instinct had been to turn to flight, but something in the tone of her voice made them pause. It was not the tone of the outraged landowner, of the Mrs. Bott who had so summarily dismissed them from her grounds earlier in the day. It was propitiatory—almost pleading. Warily, still poised for flight, they drew nearer. . . . She looked at them and gulped hysterically.

"Pardon me," she said. "I'm still feelin' *that* upset. . . . Now, boys, about that lake. I don't mind you playin' by it. I—I'd like you to play by it. Play by it as much as you like. An' if ever you see it risin' an'—an' spreadin', like—come an' tell me immediate, will you?"

William found his voice with an effort. He couldn't

"COME 'ERE, BOYS," CALLED MRS. BOTT.

understand what was happening. He'd hoped that Mrs.
Bott would not realise that it was he who had desecrated
her precious air raid shelter by pouring water into it, but
he hadn't expected this ingratiating manner, this kindly,
encouraging tone.

"Yes," he promised. "Yes, I'll come an' tell you "

"Play there whenever you like an' as long as you
like," she urged. "I don't mind a bit. I'd *like* you to.
Don't take any notice of what I said this morning. I was
only having a joke with you. An' you can come along to
our air raid shelter, too, whenever you like."

"*Can* we?" gasped Ginger.

"'Course you can," said Mrs. Bott kindly. "Come
along as often as you like. Stay as long as you like. An'—

an' if you see it lookin' damp or *watery*, you'll come an' tell me at once, won't you?"

"Yes," said Ginger faintly.

She waddled away, followed by Mr. Bott.

* * *

William and Ginger and Solrun were playing by the lake side. The adventure in the air raid shelter seemed to have restored the little girl's spirits. She ran happily about, marshalling her submarine fleet.

Mrs. Bott waddled past on her way to her A.R.P. shift. She smiled at them anxiously, encouragingly.

"Now, boys," she said, "you play 'ere as long as you like. . . . If there's anythin' you'd like done 'ere just tell me. An' pop over to 'ave a look at the shelter when you've got a minute. 'Ave a nice little game there. Doesn't matter leavin' it untidy. We can tidy it up easy enough."

She smiled at them again and waddled on.

"She's batty," said William simply, "but it's jolly good luck for us she's batty. Crumbs! It's jolly fine havin' this lake *an'* the dugout. There mightn't be a war on at all. . . ."

The little girl looked at the retreating figure of Mrs. Bott and burst into a peal of laughter.

"Oh—she—was—so—*funnee*!" she said.

Chapter 6

William and the Man from Africa

"He's from Africa," said William proudly. "I bet he's shot no end of lions."

"That aunt of yours what came from Africa," Ginger reminded him, "hadn't even *seen* one."

"I know," said William, casting his mind back to the episode of Aunt Louie, "I know, but she came from a *tamed* part. It's called Cape Town, is the tamed part, but this cousin of my father's comes from the *wild* part. The wild part's called Rhodesia, an' he comes from that. It's *full* of lions an' elephants an' buffaloes an' things, an' I bet this cousin of my father's has shot ever so many. He's prob'ly an explorer as well. . . ."

The Outlaws listened with interest. They needed something just now to restore their self-respect. The ranks of the rival gang of Hubert Laneites had been swollen recently by the addition of two stalwart youths—sons of an old school friend of Mrs. Lane, who were staying with the Lanes. Against these the Outlaws had no chance at all, and a series of ignominious defeats had left them sore both in body and spirit.

And that was not all. A camp for the unemployed had been opened in the neighbourhood, and, though most of its occupants were friendly and law-abiding, there were

among them a few formidable toughs, who took a
delight in chasing the Outlaws out of their favourite
haunts in woods and fields and lanes.

"Have you *seen* this cousin of your father's?" said
Douglas. "Is he a big man?"

"No, I've never seen him," admitted William, "but
he's big all right. All those people in that wild part of
Africa are big, all right. They've gotter be 'cause of
fightin' wild animals an' such like."

"He'll jolly well make 'em sit up, then," said Henry
with a sigh of satisfaction.

"Yes, I bet he will," said William with a short laugh.
"I bet he'll give people round here somethin' to remember, all right. I bet they'll treat us a bit diff'rent once
they've seen him."

Stories of the prowess of Mr. Brown's cousin—by
name Mr. Ticehurst—were sedulously circulated by the
Outlaws among their friends and enemies. They drew a
picture of a sort of Goliath whose path through life was
littered with the dead bodies of wild beasts and even of
his enemies.

"I bet he's killed men, too," said William darkly.
"They do out in wild countries. They don't think
anythin' of killin' men. They jus'—well, they jus' kill
'em. Yes," with a short meaning laugh, "a few of the
people round here 'll have to jolly well look out. . . ."

It was, therefore, a distinct shock, when the long
expected guest arrived, to find that he was a small
insignificant-looking man, wearing spectacles. After the
first moment of dismay, however, William quickly
adjusted himself to the situation. He remembered having heard someone say that all great men were small.
They had instanced Drake, Nelson, Napoleon, and
Julius Cæsar. They had mentioned, too, Selous, the

great elephant-hunter. So loth was William to relinquish his cherished dream that within half an hour of his arrival Mr. Ticehurst's lack of stature became added proof of his valour. The spectacles were a slight difficulty at first, but William soon decided that his eyesight had been damaged by the glare of the trackless veld, or, more probably, the charge of a rogue elephant. . . . The fact that Mr. Ticehurst, who disliked children, completely ignored him, helped, too, to restore his prestige, for William never had any great opinion of visitors who made much of him.

After dinner the visitor and Mr. Brown sat together in the study talking. Mr. Ticehurst was an insurance agent in Bulawayo, and liked to talk about insurance. The scraps of conversation overheard by William, who listened at the keyhole outside whenever he got an opportunity, were reassuring.

"I've probably taken more of that type of risk than anyone else in Africa." . . . "I admit it's dangerous but I've managed to get through all right so far." . . . "Invasion, civil war, rebellions, revolution, insurrection, military and usurped power. . . ."

"Gee whiz!" breathed William in ecstasy.

After breakfast the next morning he approached the guest with a respect that verged on reverence.

"'Scuse me, please," he said, "but, if you met a lion, a buffalo an' an elephant all chargin' at you at once, which would you shoot first?"

Mr. Ticehurst inspected William through his spectacles. A pity that the household included a child, but one generally had to pay for hospitality one way or another.

He considered the question conscientiously and impersonally. Quite impersonally, for, far from being a lion hunter, he was afraid even of dogs, and his only shooting had taken place at the age of seventeen in a booth, where, except for a tea-pot on a hoop-là stall ten yards away from the target, he had hit nothing. Still—this child had evidently been reading adventure stories and wanted a little conversation on those lines. The Browns were being exceedingly kind to him, and he must play his part as well as he could by conversing with the child on the lines chosen by the child.

"Er—the lion," he said at last.

"And then which?" said William.

"The—er—elephant."

"And then the buffalo?"

"Indubitably."

But William hadn't finished with him.

"S'pose a whole herd of elephants charged you—would you shoot 'em all?"

Mr. Ticehurst was growing tired of the conversation.

"I doubt if I should shoot them all, but the contingency is not likely to arise."

"You mean you wouldn't let 'em see you?"

"I certainly should not."

William drew a deep breath of satisfaction. He'd never had any doubts, but, if he had had, they would have vanished at this. The man shot lions, elephants, buffaloes without turning a hair. He was such a magnificent elephant stalker that he could get right up to them without any of them seeing him. . . .

He set off to join the Outlaws and share with them the reflected glory of his hero. But the Outlaws had seen Mr. Ticehurst. They had watched him arrive at the station. They had watched him climb nervously and without agility into the station cab. They had watched Mr. Brown showing him round the garden after tea. They

"I DOUBT IF I SHOULD SHOOT THEM ALL, BUT THE
CONTINGENCY IS NOT LIKELY TO ARISE," SAID MR. TICEHURST.

greeted William as indignantly as if he had deliberately
deceived them.

"Him!" said Ginger. "You said he was over six feet
high an' he's not much bigger'n me."

"You said he was so strong he'd killed a lion an' a bear

same as David," said Douglas, "an' look at him. He couldn't kill a ninsect."

"Why, he can't even *see*!" said Henry. "He's gotter wear specs!"

"No, but listen," pleaded William. "He's short, but he's *terribly* strong an' *terribly* brave. I heard him talkin' to my father las' night an' he said he'd done more dangerous things than anyone else in Africa. An' he said he'd took part in revolutions an' civil wars. An' this mornin' he told me about shootin' a lion an' a buffalo an' an elephant all at once jus' as they were chargin' him an' how he can stalk right up to elephants without them seein' him."

All this weighed for nothing, however, with the Outlaws, beside the memory of that small and weedy-looking figure that had arrived at the Browns' last night.

"Him!" said Ginger again contemptuously.

"He was pullin' your leg," said Douglas.

"He can't see to shoot anythin', not with specs like that," said Henry.

"But he got his eyes bad with an elephant chargin' at him," said William, who had by now quite persuaded himself of the truth of this. "It came chargin' at him an' kicked him right in the eye."

"He was pullin' your leg," said Douglas again. "I saw him gettin' out of the cab at your gate an' he looked scared as anythin' jus' because a motor-cyclist was comin' down the road."

"He didn't," William defended his hero stoutly, "an' all really great men are small. I heard someone sayin' so. Same as Nelson an' a man what hunted elephants. Why, this cousin of my father's—Gosh! You should hear him talk! He's been in invasions an' rebellions an' things more times than he could count."

"*Him!*" said Ginger again in terse contempt.

"Shut up sayin' 'him'," snapped William. "If you don't b'lieve me, well, I'll *prove* it to you."

"How?" said Douglas. "You can't take him lion huntin' here, 'cause there aren't any."

"I know," said William regretfully, "but"—with sudden inspiration—"there's that bull of Farmer Jenks's. It's jolly savage. Even Farmer Jenks is scared of it, an' his men won't go near it. . . . It's in the field nex' the old barn. Tell you what. I'll get this Mr. Ticehurst to go through that field with the bull in it an' then you'll see how brave he is."

The Outlaws were impressed by this offer. The bull was notoriously dangerous. It would be a test of anyone's courage to go through the field that contained it. A man used to disposing of charging elephants would, of course, make nothing of it.

"All right," they agreed. "What time'll you bring him?"

"Soon as he's had his lunch," said William. "You c'n all be there watchin' an' I bet you'll jolly well see somethin' worth seein'. Why, he's shot lions an' elephants an' buffaloes all chargin' at once."

"He won't have a gun," objected Douglas, "an' anyway he'd get in a row, shootin' Farmer Jenks's bull."

"He won't need a gun for a little thing like a bull," said William, and added darkly, "an' Farmer Jenks'd better be careful, too. When this cousin of my father's gets mad with anyone—well, they've gotter be careful, that's all. . . . I bet there's men out in Africa what knows that, all right. Small men are always more *dangerous* than big ones. Stands to reason. Their strength hasn't as much room to spread out. . . ."

After lunch, William approached Mr. Ticehurst and asked him to go for a walk with him. Mr. Ticehurst, who had intended to retire to his bedroom for a nap, sighed but acquiesced. He had paid for his breakfast by conversing with the child of the house, and now he supposed he must pay for his lunch by taking a walk with him. He'd make it as short as possible and would certainly not allow it to become a precedent. He liked his after-lunch nap and always fancied he got indigestion if he missed it. Moreover, he had felt that morning the slight pain in one ear that always heralded a cold, and he wanted to keep out of draughts as far as possible. He went upstairs slowly and reluctantly to put cotton wool in his ears and fetched his walking stick and his terai hat. The terai hat was Mr. Ticehurst's only peculiarity. He always wore it in England because he liked people to know that he came from Africa. He wore also a rather peculiar fawn and red shot sports coat, which, he explained, kept out the actinic rays of the tropical sun.

"Here I am, my boy," he said rather testily. "Now where do you want to go?"

William looked at him with approval. He liked the terai hat and he liked the tropical sports coat. His imagination had endowed the small weedy figure with such heroic qualities that it wore, in his eyes, an almost super-human air.

"Jus' a country walk," he said. "Jus' through a few fields an' things."

It had been arranged that he should not warn his hero of the presence of the bull. It was his courage and resource in the presence of unsuspected danger that was to be triumphantly vindicated under the eyes of the watching Outlaws. It never occurred to William to doubt the issue of the contest. To a man accustomed to lions, elephants and buffaloes, a bull would be child's play. . . .

He made several attempts at conversation as they went towards the old barn, but Mr. Ticehurst did not respond. His lack of response, however, only increased William's respect for him. Silent, reserved, resolute. . . . The stuff of which heroes were made.

They had reached the old barn now. William could see the heads of Ginger, Douglas and Henry peeping cautiously out as they watched the approach of the unconscious toreador. Mr. Ticehurst was wondering whether he might suggest turning back. He was afraid that walking on the grass like this would help to bring on his cold. He didn't like walking at the best of times, but, if he had to walk, he preferred walking on a road.

"D'you mind going through this field alone?" William was saying. (He didn't, of course, want to hamper Mr. Ticehurst unduly in his contest with the bull. To subdue a bull alone and unaided was one thing, but to have to rescue someone else from it at the same time was perhaps asking too much even of a man accustomed to lions and elephants.) "I want to go round by the other side of the hedge to look for a few birds' nests. I'll meet you at the stile at the other end. . . ."

Mr. Ticehurst understood this more from William's gestures than from his words, for the cotton wool in his ears made him deafer than usual. He looked without enthusiasm, first at the field (surely the grass was damp!) then at the muddy ditch in which William proposed to make his circuit. All things considered, the field was better. So intent was he on studying the grass for traces of dampness that he did not see either the notice "Beware of the Bull" that showed erratically on an overgrown hedge, or the squat muscular thick-necked figure of Farmer Jenks's bull (by name Clarence) who was watching him from under a tree in a corner of the field. He pushed the cotton wool further into his ears and stepped carefully over the stile.

"Very well, my boy," he said, "but after this," firmly, "we'll turn back, if you don't mind."

He set out across the field. To add to his discomfort, a fine drizzle had begun to fall. He slipped off his glasses and put them into his pocket. They were worse than useless when they were wet, and it was only a case of walking in a straight line across a field, at the end of which the boy would be waiting for him. He'd be very firm in future about not coming out for walks. He'd say he had letters to write. He wished he'd thought of that to-day. . . . Clarence stood watching him, pawing the ground and breathing noisily. The four Outlaws gazed at him spellbound from the other side of the hedge. Clarence advanced slowly upon the unconscious figure in the terai hat. He was in doubt whether the intruder was Farmer Jenks or not. If it were Farmer Jenks he had no intention of charging. That morning he had tried to charge Farmer Jenks, and Farmer Jenks had hit him hard and painfully on the nose with a stick. If a stranger, he must certainly charge. Clarence found that it relieved the monotony of life to charge strange people and watch them beat it like rabbits. But he wasn't sure—— Was it Farmer Jenks, or wasn't it? It wore an oddly shaped hat, but so did Farmer Jenks. No, surely it wasn't. . . . Clarence took a few paces forward and uttered a ferocious bellow. The sound, muted by cotton wool, reached Mr. Ticehurst, stepping delicately across the field and resolving some problem connected with insurance, as one of those vague and distant sounds inseparable from the life of the country-side—a cock crowing, or a horse neighing, or a cow lowing . . . certainly not that of a bull bellowing a few yards away. He continued his way without even turning round. The Outlaws watched him, open-eyed, open-mouthed with excitement. William's heart swelled with pride. "That's all bulls mean to *him*!" he said triumphantly.

Clarence repeated his bellow with the same result. He looked doubtfully at the small figure plodding so unconcernedly along. If it weren't Farmer Jenks, it should, by all the rules of the game, have been bolting like a hare to the safety of the hedge. But he felt committed now to the tactics of offence, and lowered his head for a charge. At that moment William realised suddenly the danger in which he had placed his father's guest. There he was—walking placidly along, with the bull thundering up behind him. William gave a warning yell. It happened to be on a note that penetrated the cotton wool in Mr. Ticehurst's ears. The boy hailing him, he supposed, with boylike exuberance from the other side of the hedge. . . . He turned round and raised his stick to return the greeting. Clarence dug his front feet into the ground and skidded up to within a yard of him. It *was* Farmer Jenks. No one but Farmer Jenks would swing round on him and raise his stick like that. He'd felt that stick once to-day and didn't want to feel it again. Mr. Ticehurst, having politely returned his young friend's greeting, as he thought, went on his way, intent on picking out the driest spots, still unaware of Clarence sidling along uncertainly behind him. He had reached the stile now and placed his foot on the lowest rung. Clarence debated whether to charge the stile, but, remembering that stiles hurt almost as much as sticks, decided not. Suddenly he saw a small boy half-way through the hedge. It was a providential opportunity for

MR. TICEHURST TURNED ROUND AND RAISED HIS STICK TO
RETURN THE GREETING.

face-saving. He turned and charged violently. Ginger
just got back in time. . . .

Mr. Ticehurst climbed down slowly and carefully from
the stile. The boy was there waiting for him with three
friends. They were staring at him as if there was something odd about him. It irritated Mr. Ticehurst. The rain
had stopped, so he took out his spectacles and put them

on again. Glancing round he thought he saw a cow in a corner of the field he had just come through and shivered slightly. A good thing he hadn't seen it before. He'd always been nervous of cows. . . .

"Well! Well! Well!" he said. "Come, come, come! Let's get home."

The boys all followed him—still staring at him in that peculiar way.

* * *

"Well, you saw, didn't you?" said William proudly. "You saw, all right. Jus' turned an' put his stick up at it. That's all he did. An' it stopped right in the middle of chargin'. P'raps you'll believe now that he shot all those lions an' things."

The Outlaws certainly believed. They had seen his calm and masterly exhibition of bull-taming with their own eyes. They apologised. They ate their words. He was everything that William said he was.

"Wish those Hubert Laneites had seen," said Ginger wistfully.

"Yes, wish he could have a go at *them*," said Douglas. "I'd jolly well like to see him havin' a go at *them*."

"Well, why shun't he?" said William. "Why shun't he have a go at 'em? Tell you what. Let's—let's fix it."

They fixed it. The plot was carefully laid. They were to call for Mr. Ticehurst the next morning and take him for a walk. They were to approach the spot where the Laneites usually forgathered. All of them were to go forward but one, who was to delay Mr. Ticehurst till the advance party was engaged in hostilities in which they would inevitably get the worst of it, and then, at the psychological moment, bring him forward to avenge them and give the Laneites the thrashing of their lives.

The scheme involved some self-sacrifice on the part of the advance party, who would get badly knocked about until the reinforcements arrived. William decided to lead the advance party. Ginger was deputed to hold back the bull-tamer till the time was ripe for him to appear in the shape of a human Nemesis.

At first everything went according to plan. Mr. Ticehurst agreed reluctantly to accompany them on a walk. He didn't want to, but he was a conscientious man and there was no doubt that the Browns were doing him well. The bed was a comfortable one, the meals were punctual and well cooked, and Brown let him talk insurance to his heart's content, which was more than some people did. The cold that had seemed to be threatening yesterday hadn't yet materialised, but he was still afraid that it might. The country was always damp and draughty, and one could so easily get overheated by hurrying unduly. There was, therefore, no difficulty in keeping him back while the others went on to the spot where the Laneites were assembled. The two stalwarts were there and as soon as the Outlaws appeared fell on them with re-echoing war whoops. There was no chivalry about the Laneites. They only fought, in fact, when the odds were heavily on their side. The advance party suffered, but it suffered gladly, believing that retribution was at hand.

It was at this point that things went wrong. Ginger, recognising the sounds of battle, hastened his companion.

"I say!" he said, in well simulated surprise and curiosity. "What's all that noise? Let's go 'n' see what's happenin'."

The next bend in the path showed them what was happening, showed the Hubert Laneites, with the two stalwarts at their head, dealing destruction right and left upon the Outlaws.

Ginger looked at Mr. Ticehurst in happy confidence. The long expected moment of triumph had arrived. . . . But apparently it hadn't. Mr. Ticehurst stood motionless, surveying the scene with growing distaste. Boys. . . . Rough untidy boys. . . . Boys fighting and punching each other's heads. . . . A disgusting exhibition of hooliganism. . . . He was sorry he'd let them persuade him to come out for a walk with them. He'd always disliked boys. . . . They were nothing more or less than savages. . . . Look at them now . . . punching, wrestling, shouting. . . .

"Tut! tut!" said Mr. Ticehurst. "Dear, dear, dear!" and with that turned and hurried away from the distressing scene.

Ginger gaped after him. At first he couldn't believe that their destined protector had deserted them, that their bull-taming hero was no hero, after all. He even thought for a moment that Mr. Ticehurst must have gone to fetch a weapon in order to protect his friends from their foes more effectively, but there was no mistaking the single purpose of flight written all over the small, swiftly departing figure. Ginger turned to take part in the fray half-heartedly. The Outlaws, hopelessly outnumbered, were routed from the field.

*   *   *

"Him!" said Ginger again contemptuously. "Bet he's never *seen* a lion!"

"There we went," said Douglas bitterly, "gettin' ourselves knocked about all over the place—I c'n hardly move without it hurting even now—jus' so's he could come in an' smash 'em up, an' what does he do? Runs

BOYS . . . ROUGH UNTIDY BOYS. . . . BOYS FIGHTING AND
PUNCHING EACH OTHER'S HEADS. . . . A DISGUSTING
EXHIBITION OF HOOLIGANISM. . . .

away! That's what he does!"

"P'raps he didn't see," said William in feeble defence
of his late hero.

"See!" said Ginger indignantly. "'Course he saw!
'Tut, tut!' he said, an' 'Dear, dear, dear!' an' off he went
quick as he could, 'case someone hit him."

"He's a mean ole coward, that's what he is," said
Henry, stroking a black eye tenderly. "A rotten, mean,
ole cowardy custard!"

"Well, he didn't run away from that bull," said

"TUT! TUT!" SAID MR. TICEHURST. "DEAR! DEAR!"
AND WITH THAT TURNED AND HURRIED AWAY FROM THE
DISTRESSING SCENE.

William, to whom this reflection was the sole ray of light in a dark and gloomy situation.

"*Bull!*" echoed Ginger scornfully. "I bet he didn't even know it was a bull. Bet he thought it was a cow all the time. Bet he didn't even *see* it. He's as blind as a bat even with his specs, an' he'd took his specs off goin' across that field."

"Not that he'd have done much good if he *had* come in," said Henry. "He couldn't hit a fly."

"*Him!*" said Ginger again in withering contempt.

"Him an' *lions*. I don't think!"

"Oh, shut up!" said William. "I'm sick of him."

"Yes, an' so are we all," said Douglas, "an' we'll be sicker before we've finished. *They* saw him all right an' they won't forget in a hurry."

That indeed was the bitterest part of the pill. The Hubert Laneites had heard of the vaunted prowess of Mr. Brown's cousin, slayer of lions, tamer of bulls— William had been as good as a loud speaker in this respect—and now they had seen the hero with their own eyes, had seen him appear on the field of action, seen him blench and shrink at the sight of violence, seen the stricken glance he threw them as he turned to flight. . . . Douglas was right. There was not much likelihood of their forgetting. One of them had even overheard the "Tut, tut! Dear, dear, dear!"

"Tut, tut!" they jeered. "Dear, dear, dear! I can see some nasty rough boys fightin'. Oh dear! I mus' run home. I'm so frightened of boys."

They refused now even to accept the Outlaws' version of the bull affair.

"Who was chased by a cow?" they jeered. "*Yah!*"

The Outlaws blamed William for their downfall.

"Him!" said Ginger scornfully for the hundredth time. "I bet those elephants never saw him at all. I bet they thought he was a rabbit."

"All right," said William. "All *right*. I don't care. I've finished with him, anyway. I don't care what he does or where he goes or anythin' about him."

And so William proceeded to ignore Mr. Ticehurst and his doings completely. This was rather a mistake, for Mr. Ticehurst's doings during the next few days might have interested him. Mr. Ticehurst was, on his side, glad to be relieved of the company of William and his friends.

He resumed the even tenor of his ways and took an occasional gentle stroll in the evening along the lanes, carefully avoiding field paths because of the damp. It was on one of these gentle strolls that his next adventure befell him. He found himself suddenly surrounded by half a dozen extremely unpleasant-looking men. He tried to hurry on, but, without actually laying hands on him, they managed to bar his way. Despite their threatening appearance they were quite polite. They said it was a nice evening and asked him how he was. He said that he was very well and tried to pass through them. He found himself gently pushed back. The largest and most unpleasant-looking of the group then told him that they were starting a Benevolent Fund among themselves and asked him if he would like to contribute to it. At first Mr. Ticehurst said, "Certainly not," but the group closed in on him, and the big man put his face right up to his and said wouldn't he like to reconsider it. Mr. Ticehurst hastily reconsidered it. He handed the big man half a crown. The big man thanked him, but said that they'd like a larger subscription if he was sure he could spare it. Mr. Ticehurst took out his note-case with trembling fingers and handed him a ten-shilling note. It was a foolish action, for it revealed the fact that the case contained several other notes—ten shilling and pound. The group pressed upon him more closely still. The big man, looking more threatening than ever, said surely he could spare a little more for such a deserving cause. Mr. Ticehurst would have called for help, but he was past calling for anything. His throat was dry and his knees unsteady. He was wondering whether his dead body would be found in the lane to-morrow morning or whether his brutal murderers would have disposed of it. At each note he handed out they let him take a step forward before they closed in on him again.

Not till the case was empty did they leave him. With their departure Mr. Ticehurst's courage returned in a rush. He was furious. He could hardly contain his anger. That this—*this*—should have happened to a peaceable citizen in a country where law and order were supposed to prevail! Seething with indignation, he made his way to the police station. Entering it like a miniature tempest, he bumped into a smallish man just coming out. So violent was the impact that Mr. Ticehurst was thrown on to his back in the road. It was the last straw. Never in all his life had he felt so near bursting into tears. . . .

"Beg pardon," said the man, as he helped Mr. Ticehurst to his feet. He was a genial-looking little man, with a flashy tie-pin and a garish many-coloured tie. "If that ain't me all over! Come and sit down on the seat till you get your wind back."

He led Mr. Ticehurst to a wooden bench by the roadside on which the village ancients sat in the evening to watch the traffic go by.

"If that ain't me all over!" he repeated with a hearty laugh. "Yuman Tornado they used to call me in the ring an' Yuman Tornado I still am."

"Ring?" said Mr. Ticehurst testily, brushing the dust from his suit. "Why don't you look where you're going? What ring? What are you talking about?"

"Boxing ring," said the man. "Light weight champion I was. Jimmy Hayes, the 'uman Tornado."

Artlessly expansive, Jimmy proceeded to relate his history—his many triumphs, his gradual realisation that his day as a champion was over and his recent achievement of a long standing ambition to be a barman in a country pub.

"Git out in time, that's my motter," he said. "No 'anging on. I'm as good a boxer as *you're* ever likely to meet, but I'm not championship form no longer—so 'Git out of it, Jimmy,' I sez to myself. 'Get out while the goin's good, as they say.' So that when folks think of me they'll think of me as the 'uman Tornado—not as a mouldy ole 'as-been draggin' round the ring. . . . Seen too much of that in me time. I'd 'ave bought a pub if I'd 'ad the money. Money? Gosh! It's flowed through me 'ands like water. Easy come, easy go, with me. Never could keep it. What's money for, anyway? To spend while you 'ave it, I sez, not to 'old on to. Got a nice snug berth at the Red Lion now, too. All the same, mind you, the country's not so innercent as what it's cracked up to be in po'try. 'Ad me pocket-book stole off me this mornin'. Ten bob it 'ad in it. Jus' been in there," he cocked his thumb towards the police station, "to tell 'em. Fat lot o' good it'll do. They never puts themselves out for anythin' 'cept their meals.''

Mr. Ticehurst, who had been bored by Jimmy's personal history, became interested at this.

"Do I understand that you have been robbed, too?" he said, adjusting his spectacles.

"You do," said Jimmy grimly. "Ten blinkin' bob I've bin robbed of.''

"Did they ask you to—er—contribute to a Benevolent Fund?" asked Mr. Ticehurst.

The Human Tornado stared at him.

"Benevolent Fund? Wotcher mean? Down in 'Adley it 'appened. Comin' out of the pitchers. . . . Benevolent Fund? What's that got to do with it?''

Ordinarily, Mr. Ticehurst would not have dreamed of confiding his troubles in this common little man, but he was still feeling upset, and there was about the Human Tornado something that inspired confidence. Though small, one felt that he would be equal to most occasions.

He listened carefully to Mr. Ticehurst's indignant recital.

"I see," he said at last. "Well, you'll never get *them*," he jerked his thumb again towards the police station door, "to take it up. All red tape, that's what they are. Brought up on it from babies. Bet you twopence they say there's nothin' to make a case out of, that they asked you for money an' you gave it 'em. No, a thing like that's best settled private. Don't suppose you c'n get your money back, but what you want to do is to teach 'em a lesson they won't forget in a hurry."

"Indeed, I do," said Mr. Ticehurst, trembling with anger at the memory of the outrage perpetrated on him. "Indeed, I do! And I have hopes that, despite what you say, the police will take the matter up."

"Don't you worry, they won't," said Jimmy. "I know 'em. Gotter break a lor to smithereens before they'll as much as raise a finger. An' what lors there is is easy enough got round. I know," he admitted modestly, "'cause I've got round a good few myself in my time. . . . No, what you oughter do is to let me give you a few lessons. I'll make a special price. Five shillin's a lesson, that's all I'll charge you. Five shillings a lesson from the 'uman Tornado, an' if that's not dirt cheap I don't know what is. Then, when you've 'ad a few lessons, you can go out again an' let 'em try it on again an' show 'em a thing or two. Why, there's men I've taught what's well on the way to a championship now. . . . Dirt cheap, it is, at five shillings an hour."

Mr. Ticehurst had turned pale.

"No, no," he said. "Of course not. I couldn't dream . . . Nothing would induce me——"

The Human Tornado was looking at him speculatively.

"Very well," he said. "Just as you please. P'raps it wouldn't be much use. I've got a better plan than that——"

"What?" said Mr. Ticehurst.

"You go in an' see what the cops 'ave to say, an', if you don't get no satisfaction from them, I'll tell you this other plan of mine."

Mr. Ticehurst entered the police station and emerged a few moments later, tense with indignation.

"Outrageous!" he spluttered. "Simply outrageous! They say they can take no action. They *know* the men, they say, and know that they're bad lots, but they say that on my evidence no action can be taken. It's—it's—it's—it's *outrageous*. To think that such scoundrels should get off scot free! It's—*outrageous*."

"They won't get off scot free," the Human Tornado assured him. "I'll tell you my plan. . . ."

*   *   *

"I wish he'd go," said William despondently. "They might forget if he'd go. He's been here nearly a week. I'm sick of the sight of him."

The Outlaws were walking across a field towards a stile that led into the road.

"Wish those two boys stayin' with Hubert Lane'd go, too," grumbled Ginger. "I'm sick of bein' chased by them. An' the way they keep on about him. On an' on an' on—— Think it's funny singin' out 'Who ran away from a fight?' every time they see us. An' 'Who was chased by a cow?' "

"It was a bull, an' he *did* tame it all right," said William, rising half-heartedly again to the defence of his one-time hero.

"Well, why——" began Ginger, then grabbed hold of

William and pulled him down with a whispered warning.

They had reached the lane, and Ginger had seen the band of toughs from the unemployed camp hanging about in the shadow of the trees. They watched, fascinated.

"Bet they'd murder us if they found us," whispered William, pleasurably thrilled by the idea.

Suddenly he saw Hubert Lane and the two stalwarts coming down the lane. Seeing the toughs, they, too, dived through the hedge on the opposite side of the road, taking cover in the field. Laneites and Outlaws looked at each other through the double barrier of hedges, but the greater danger in the space between kept them apart.

"Let's get back a bit," they heard Hubert saying nervously. "They might see us."

"Coo!" said one of the stalwarts with relish, "I bet they're plottin' a crime. . . ."

At that moment a small figure in the familiar terai hat and tropical sports coat appeared at the end of the lane. It walked along slowly and deliberately as if lost in meditation. The toughs watched it silently, still standing in the shadow of the trees. Outlaws and Laneites commented excitedly:

"They'll murder him, all right."

"No, they'll only rob him."

"They won't even do that. He'll run off too quick when he sees them."

"Funny he doesn't see 'em. He's walkin' straight into 'em."

"He's thinkin' of somethin' else. He'll run off all right soon as he does."

"Look! Gosh! They're settin' on him."

But the toughs had only encircled the small figure,

who gave a start of surprise as if seeing them for the first time. The toughs closed round him and appeared to be arguing with him. The small figure waved them aside and tried to continue on his way. The toughs barred his progress. The leader held out one hand and laid the other threateningly on the tropical sports coat. Suddenly Outlaws and Laneites sprang to their feet and hung excitedly over the hedge, open-mouthed with amazement. The leader of the toughs had apparently been struck by something. He seemed to leap backwards, then fell full length on the ground. His fall revealed the small figure in a boxing attitude, his left slightly advanced, his feet moving in quick dancing steps. Neither Outlaws nor Laneites ever forgot the scene that followed. The little figure in the terai hat seemed to dance round in circles, and whenever he danced men fell down. They climbed to their feet and rushed forward only to fall down again like so many ninepins. Within three minutes the whole lot of them were fleeing down the road. The small figure watched them till they had vanished from sight, then turned slowly to retrace his steps.

Outlaws and Laneites climbed through the hedge into the now empty lane. They all stared at William humbly, almost reverently.

"Coo!" said Hubert. "Six of 'em. I counted. Six of 'em. An' he sent 'em all flyin'."

The stalwarts could only gasp amazedly.

"Gosh! I wish I'd gotter punch like that," they said wistfully.

William had quickly recovered his poise.

"I knew he was like that all along," he said. "Din' I *tell* you? Din' I tell you about that bull?"

"Yes," said Hubert, "but——"

The thoughts of all of them went to the fight from which Mr. Ticehurst had withdrawn so precipitately. They saw the explanation clearly enough now. As if a man who could knock out half a dozen great ruffians simultaneously would condescend to join in a kids' fight!

"He doesn't fight *boys*," said William. "Not a man like him. . . ."

"No," agreed the stalwarts with humility. "No, of course not. . . ."

It was the day of Mr. Ticehurst's departure. The Outlaws were going to the station to see him off. Mr. Ticehurst did not want to be seen off by the Outlaws. He had found the attentions of the Outlaws during the past few days acutely embarrassing. They followed him about wherever he went, staring at him. They waited on him hand and foot, offering to carry things for him, fetching things for him that he didn't want, opening doors and gates for him. . . . At one time he thought he had noticed a distinct lack of respect in the way those boys looked at him and spoke to him, but for the last few days he had had nothing to complain of on that score. They still stared at him a good deal, but it was certainly not a disrespectful stare. One of them had asked him yesterday what was the best diet for a boxer, and when he said he knew nothing about boxing they had all laughed as if he had made a joke. . . .

His mind went back over the visit. Nice kind people, the Browns, and the boy's manners had improved considerably towards the end. He still felt hot with indignation when he remembered the assault made on his notecase by the toughs from the unemployed camp. Though he had informed the police, he had not mentioned the matter to his hosts, as he felt that he figured in the incident in a somewhat ignominious light. He still considered that Jimmy Hayes had charged him too much for that little boxing exhibition. Two pounds was a lot on the top of what the men had taken from him. But on the whole he didn't regret it. It had certainly been a pleasant experience to see the men slink away from him apprehensively the next time he wandered past the camp.

The Outlaws stood round him on the platform possessively, aware of the Hubert Laneites snatching a less privileged last glance of the hero from the road outside the station. They were admiring not only that never-to-be-forgotten exhibition of boxing, but the modest gentle bearing of their idol. To watch him, to hear him talk, you would never think that he scattered mighty men with one movement of his arm. Of such stuff, of course, were heroes made. . . .

The days since the great fight had been like a dream to the Outlaws. Once more their beloved fields and woods, and lanes were theirs, unchallenged. The toughs from the camp gave them free passage. The Laneites were their followers and slaves. In exchange for details of Mr. Ticehurst's diet and daily routine even the stalwarts would eat dirt.

"What time does he get up in the morning?" . . . "What does he have for his breakfast?" . . . "What time does he go to bed?"

Haughtily, condescendingly, patronisingly, the Outlaws doled out bits of information. And to-morrow the stalwarts were going home, and the day after that the camp was breaking up.

The train came in. The porter put Mr. Ticehurst's bag on the rack. Mr. Ticehurst slipped a half-crown into William's hand.

"Well, my boy," he said in his rather high-pitched,

precise voice, "goodbye. . . . I've had a very pleasant visit."

"Good-bye," said the Outlaws, still fixing him with that embarrassing stare. (They wanted to impress every feature of the great man on their memories.)

"Goodbye——"

The train steamed away into the distance. The Outlaws stood watching till it had disappeared, then turned and went out of the station. Immediately the waiting Laneites closed round them—no longer in hostility, but humbly, appealingly.

"Go on, William," said Hubert. "Tell us about him chasin' those bulls again. . . ."

For the bull episode was now not only fully credited but had been exaggerated beyond recognition.

"Tell us what he has for tea," pleaded a stalwart. "Gosh! I shall never forget him goin' for 'em. . . ."

"What did he say when he said good-bye?" asked Bertie Franks.

"All right," said William, assuming a haughty dictatorial air. "All right. I can't tell you everythin' at once. Give me a little room to walk, can't you?" Respectfully they drew away from him. "I can't tell you what he said when he said good-bye 'cause it was private, but for tea yesterday he had——"

Crowding round him, drinking in his words, they accompanied him home. . . .

Chapter 7

William and the Black-Out

William wanted a tin hat. All the other Outlaws, all the other boys he knew, had tin hats of one sort or another, but it so happened that William was without either a tin hat or the money to buy one. Very inferior ones could be bought for as little as sixpence in Hadley, but William did not want an inferior one, and in any case he did not possess sixpence. The one he wanted cost one and six, but he was as likely to have the moon as one and six, he told himself, adding with bitter sarcasm, "a jolly sight likelier". His pocket money was mortgaged for a month to come in order to pay for the crockery he had broken while training to be a juggler. "Well, they've all gotter learn, haven't they?" he had protested, when sentence was passed on him. "Gosh! D'you think jugglers can throw up plates like that without practisin'? D'you think they're *born* throwin' up plates like that? They've gotter break a few plates an' things practisin'. Stands to reason. . . . Well, how'm I goin' to earn my livin' bein' a juggler when I'm grown up if you won't let me practise? Anyone 'd think you didn't *want* me to earn my livin' when I'm grown up. It's goin' to be jolly expensive to you keepin' me all my life, just 'cause you won't ever let me start practisin' to earn my livin' jugglin' . . ."

Hearing his father's key in the lock, he had decided to cut short the argument and had gone out into the garden, where he sat on an upturned wheelbarrow and threw stones at the next door cat, who sat unmoved on the fence, eyeing him sardonically. . . .

"I might be killed in an air raid any minute without it," he explained indignantly to the cat, throwing a stone that went about a foot wide, "an' a fat lot they'd care!"

Having indulged his self-pity to the top of its bent, he set to work to ponder ways and means. His father he did not even consider as a possible donor of the tin hat. His father was, in his opinion, the meanest man who ever walked the earth, grumbling at school bills and clothes bills and jumping eagerly at any and every excuse for docking William of his pocket money. His mother was not quite so mean, but just now, with the loss of half a set of her best dinner plates still rankling, was not in a fit state of mind to be approached. Ethel? Ethel, in a V.A.D. uniform of extreme chicness, that did not conform to any of the known rules for V.A.D. uniforms, her cap hidden beneath a mass of curls, trotted off every day on very un-regulation high heels to her clinic and lived in a world of real and imaginary casualties. At first William had earned a few pence by letting her experiment on him with bandages and tourniquets and splints, but she had passed that stage now and was interested chiefly in more abstruse disabilities in which William could not assist her. Moreover, William was in disfavour with her at the moment, having borrowed her webbing tourniquet for the foundation of a Red Indian head dress and lost it in the wood.

Robert? Robert's affairs were always worth study, but William, considering them closely, could see little hope of a tin hat in them. Below military age, Robert was putting in time during his college vacation by taking shifts at the local A.R.P. centre. He sallied forth, splendidly warlike with tin hat and civilian duty respirator, and spent his eight hours reading thrillers or playing games with the rest of the workers. In this service to his country he was acquiring a fine technique in draughts and had already learnt several new kinds of patience. William had, of course, made many attempts on Robert's tin hat, but Robert, finding William one day trying it on, had complained to Mr. Brown, and William was now forbidden even to touch it.

"Can't even practise wearin' it," he muttered indignantly to a variegated laurel bush (the cat, disgusted by the inaccuracy of his aim, had now vanished). "Can't even practise *wearin'* it. . . . Well, what's to happen, I'd like to know, if I'm the only one left to stop a raid an' I've never even practised wearin' it? Nice thing that'll be . . . an' it'll be *his* fault. . . ."

Robert, of course, didn't spend all his time at the A.R.P. centre. In between his shifts he carried on his normal activities, and William, more for something to do than because he thought that they would really yield him a tin hat, began to study Robert's normal activities. His friendship with Philippa Pomeroy had lasted longer than his friendships with girls generally lasted. It had begun inauspiciously enough with the begging letter episode, but it had triumphantly survived a summer of constant meetings at tennis, of picnics on the river, and various other idyllic occupations that generally exhaust even the most faithful of attachments. It was therefore something of a surprise to William to realise, on turning his close attention to Robert's affairs, that, despite the tin hat and civilian duty respirator, Robert was gradually being ousted from his position as Philippa's best friend. His supplanter, William discovered, was a young man called Claude Brading, whose parents had just taken a house in Marleigh. They were reputed to be rich, and Claude, a large but somewhat pasty youth, had all the airs (if not the graces) of a man-about-town. There was no doubt that Philippa found him a refreshing change from Robert. She liked Robert and knew that he meant well, but there was nothing of the man-about-town in Robert. He was shy, gauche, and almost incredibly unsophisticated. He hadn't any small talk. His long worshipping silences had for some time now been getting on her nerves. On the other hand, Claude was doing nothing for his country beyond giving the gardener inaccurate information on the growing of vegetables (which the gardener wisely ignored) and reluctantly agreeing to make his breakfast off two rashers of bacon instead of four, while Robert had at least the tin hat and civilian duty respirator to his credit and was impatiently waiting his turn to be "called up". Still—Claude had a way with him, a self possession, a drawl, a habit of referring casually to important people and events, a general air of belonging to a larger world than the one in which he now found himself. Before coming to live in the country, Philippa had had many young men of that sort. She had thought she was tired of them, but, meeting Claude, she wasn't so sure. . . .

It happened that, the week before, William had had to take a note from Robert to Philippa telling her that he couldn't come to tea, as he had to change his A.R.P. shift, and had met Claude Brading in the Pomeroy drawing-room. William had greeted him with that grim ferocity that he fondly imagined to be the last word in politeness.

"So sorry your brother can't come," said Claude, winking at Philippa over William's head.

"Yes," said William, "he's sorry, too."

"Then we're all sorry," said Claude. "I'm sure Miss Pomeroy is," and he winked at Philippa again.

"Yes," agreed William.

He sat down hopefully on a chair between them. It was about tea time, and you generally got a jolly decent tea in other people's houses, much better than you ever got at home. He looked from one to the other cheerfully, ready to play his social part and take his share in any conversation that might be going.

"I'm sure your friends are missing you," said Claude.

"Yes, I 'spect they are," agreed William pleasantly.

There was a short silence, then Claude said:

"I can't tell you how much we enjoy having you here, but I don't think we ought to deprive your friends any longer of the pleasure of your company."

There was nothing subtle about William. He took things at their face value.

"Oh, no, that's all right," he said, flattered by the compliment. "I c'n stay here as long as you want me. I c'n stay," hopefully, "anyway till after tea."

"How splendid for us!" said Claude.

William's heart warmed to him. It wasn't often that he was welcomed to people's tea tables as cordially as this. He wished to show as much interest in Claude as Claude was so kindly showing in him.

"When are you goin' to join the army?" he asked, making polite conversation.

For a moment Claude looked a little taken aback, then: "Soon," he said airily. "Quite soon."

"What are you goin' into?" said William, still anxious to show interest in his new friend.

"I'M SURE YOUR FRIENDS ARE MISSING YOU," SAID CLAUDE.

Claude noticed that Philippa's eyes were fixed on him as if she, too, were awaiting the answer to the question.

"Well," he said. "I had thought of joining the R.A.F."

"Why don't you, then?" asked William, inspired solely by a desire to repay Claude's flattering interest.

"Well," said Claude airily, "people are enlisting in such numbers that it would be a long time before I got out to France. I should like to help more quickly than that. . . . It's solely patriotism that has stopped my enlisting in the R.A.F."

William was gazing at him in simple admiration, but there was something in Philippa's eye that Claude didn't

"YES, I 'SPECT THEY ARE," AGREED WILLIAM PLEASANTLY.

quite like. He leapt at once into a series of anecdotes illustrative of his pluck and daring. There did not seem to be a single school or college friend whom he had not at some time or other rescued from death at the risk of his own life, a single deed calling for skill, courage and resource that he had not at some time or other performed. It was, in fact, difficult to imagine how he had found time to pursue his studies during this breathlessly heroic career. . . . But it went down well with Philippa. The look of doubt vanished from her eyes and a look of admiration took its place. William gaped at him, deeply impressed. Here was a hero after his own heart, a daring fighter against odds, a noble defender of the weak and helpless, a wholesale rescuer of lives. While making a satisfactorily large tea, he drank in every detail eagerly—"six to one against me" . . . "managed to bring him to land" . . . "grasped the creature by the horns". Even when Claude himself had tired of the repertoire, William was hungrily lapping it up, asking for more. Claude then proceeded to "quizz" him in superior amused fashion in order to entertain Philippa—asking him how on earth he managed to keep so clean, and tidy, expressing surprise at the smallness of his appetite, saying again and again what a pleasure it was to meet him. William continued to take it all in good faith. He expanded in what he took to be an atmosphere of kindliness and good fellowship. He ate a lot and talked a lot, and when he took his leave was highly gratified by Claude's saying: "Well, come again some time and bring a friend."

That, then, was the situation as regards Robert. He was playing a losing game with Claude for Philippa's attention. He couldn't compete with Claude's air of sophistication and tales of valour and, though he was helping with the A.R.P., the only stories of prowess he had to relate in that connection were of battles won on the darts board, of tense moments at draughts, of hairbreadth escapes at rummy, and the technique of difficult patience games finally mastered. Moreover, his somewhat crude depreciation of his rival merely annoyed Philippa, while Claude's scornfully amused references to "our worthy young hero of the A.R.P." made Philippa see Robert in that slightly ridiculous light in which, one must admit, it was only too easy to see him.

William, reviewing the situation from every angle, decided that it could not help him much. Of the two rivals, indeed, he felt that Claude was the more deserving, for certainly Robert had never performed any deeds of daring to compare with Claude's. He made a feeble attempt to turn this situation to his advantage by offering to invent a few deeds of daring for Robert, but Robert's responses were so unencouraging that he decided to wash his hands of the whole affair.

"All right," he said distantly, "if you don't want me to help you, I won't."

"I certainly don't," said Robert. "It's the last thing in the world I want. Help indeed! I've never known *you* help anyone yet."

"All *right*," said William. "All I wanted to do was to tell her a few tales about you doin' the same sort of thing he does—savin' people an' attackin' wild animals an' such like. I bet I c'n tell 'em as well as what he does. I bet I'd make her think a bit more of you. Well, stands to reason she can't think much of you, not savin' anyone's life when he's saved dozens an' dozens. Why, when he was only five years old he went into a burnin' house what the firemen daren't go into to rescue his caterpillars, an' las' year he——"

"Shut up," said Robert between his teeth.

"All right, but you won't listen to me. I keep tellin' you, all I want to do is to help you. An' if you like to give me a tin hat for helpin' you, I don't mind. There's a jolly good one in the village for one an' six, but you c'n get 'em for a shillin' an' for sixpence. Look here, for one an' six I'll tell her you rescued ten people from a fire, an' for a shillin' I'll tell her you rescued five people from a lion, an' for sixpence I'll tell her you rescued two people from drownin'.''

Robert, scowling ferociously over a picture paper (which he held upside down), breathed heavily but gave no other sign of having heard.

William sighed.

"Well, look here, Robert," he said at last, in a tone of sweet reasonableness, "I don't want to charge you too much. A penny'd be jolly useful to me. Look here, for a penny I'll tell her that you climbed half-way down a precipice and rescued a dog what'd got stuck when it was chasin' rabbits (he's rescued hundreds of dogs), or that you climbed up a chimney to rescue a sweep what'd got stuck at the top, or that you fought a herd of wild animals what were attackin' a poor ole man. I don't want to be mean. I'll tell her any of those for a penny. I'll tell her," with a sudden inspiration, "seven of them for sixpence. That's *givin'* you one. An' I'll make it a specially good one about swimmin' up a weir or somethin' like that. . . ."

Robert twisted up the picture paper and rose, his face set and furious.

"You dare *mention* me to her, you little wretch," he said, "and I'll wring your dirty little neck."

With that he strode off, leaving William staring after him indignantly.

"Cheek!" he muttered, stroking the maligned member tenderly. "When I washed it yesterday *an'* the day before! I only didn't this mornin' 'cause I got up too late. An' anyway it stays clean for days. I've often tried it.

bet it's as clean as what his is. . . . An' I wouldn't help him now, not if he *wanted* me to."

Having washed his hands of Robert's affairs, he turned his attention to such activities as the war had left him. As a matter of fact, the war had not been without its brighter side for the Outlaws. Grown-up vigilance was modified, rules were suspended, discipline relaxed.

"You must look after yourselves," said parents, rushing off to perform their various war duties. "I really haven't time to bother with you just now."

And so the Outlaws had discovered the possibilities of the black-out. They were, of course, not supposed to go out during the black-out, but each parent was ready enough to suppose that his particular son was safe in the house of another parent, and so the Outlaws roamed the countryside unhindered in its thrilling new unlighted condition. They formed bands and tracked each other down. They occasionally leapt out from behind trees to terrify nervous pedestrians, they pushed each other into ditches, they narrowly missed being run over several times a night and had given heart attacks to innumerable motorists.

It was about a week after William's interview with Robert that William, Ginger and Henry found themselves wandering down the darkened road, having for the moment exhausted their fund of ideas. They had pushed each other into the ditch, chased each other across the fields, lost each other in the dark and found each other again, tried to frighten a postman and instead been soundly cuffed, and done their excellent (but by now too well known) imitation of an air raid warning siren without any result beyond threats from several householders to complain to their fathers the next morning.

Suddenly Ginger said:

"There's someone comin'. Let's hide."

They crouched beneath the hedge and saw a dim figure, unrecognisable in the darkness, walking quickly along the "blacked-out" road.

"Let's follow him an' see where he's goin'," whispered Henry.

"All right," said William, and they proceeded to follow the figure in single file down the road.

Claude Brading walked quickly, glancing fearfully into the shadows as he walked. He was scared stiff. Despite his endless repertoire of rescue stories, no more timorous soul than Claude Brading existed. He was afraid of lonely country roads even in broad daylight. A country road in the black-out petrified him. He had been to tea with Philippa and now had to walk two miles home. He wasn't used to walking in any circumstances. Generally the parental car fetched him from his engagements, but it happened that it had been telephoned for at the last moment to meet his father at the station. He had walked to Philippa's in the daylight, and he hadn't realised that the black-out was quite as black as this. . . .

Moreover, the conversation at Philippa's had been peculiarly disturbing. It had dealt with stories of robberies, assaults and even murders, committed during the black-out. To judge from the stories which the guests exchanged, anyone who ventured on a journey— however short—during the black-out was lucky if he reached the end of it alive. Even the most optimistic could hardly expect to reach it without having everything he had on him stolen. . . . His teeth chattered as he walked and occasionally he muttered to himself, making pleas for mercy to imaginary assailants. . . .

Suddenly a figure stepped out of the shadow and raised a stick.

"Don't!" groaned Claude. "Don't! Here take this, It's all I have. . . ."

In trembling haste he pulled out three ten-shilling notes, a cigarette-case and a note-book, thrust them into the other man's hand, and set off to run as fast as he could down the darkened road. . . . When he had gone a few yards he stopped, pulled off his wrist watch and flung it behind him with a high-pitched "Take it!" The man took out a torch and gazed in astonishment at the haul. The Outlaws, crouching in the shadows, recognised him. It was Harry Dare, a famous local poacher. Over his shoulder was a sack containing two rabbits and a hen pheasant. Coming suddenly upon an unexpected figure in the darkness, as he emerged from the wood, he had dropped his bag and raised his stick in timorous self-defence, thinking that his old enemy, the gamekeeper, had run him to earth at last. The handful of miscellaneous articles thrust suddenly into his hand was a complete mystery to him. His first impulse was to throw them all away, but the temptation of the three ten-shilling notes was too much for him. He thrust them into his pocket, threw the cigarette-case and note-book on to the ground, shouldered his sack, and set off homewards.

The Outlaws came out of their hiding place, shaking with laughter.

"Gosh! that was funny," said William. "That was *jolly* funny! Fancy being frightened of ole Harry Dare! Wish I knew who it was. I'd have some fun with him, all right. Did you see who it was?"

But neither Ginger nor Henry had seen who it was.

"Bet that Mr. Brading'd have a good laugh over it," said William with a chuckle. "Why, he said that once he was attacked on a lonely road by a gang of men what wanted to rob him an' he jus' knocked 'em all down one after the other and walked on."

- "Why din' they get up an' run after him?" demanded Ginger.

"They were stunned," explained William simply. "Stunned. All of 'em. He can do that, jus' stun a man with one blow. It's a knack, he says. I'm goin' to get him to teach me it. . . . Gosh, he'll have a jolly good laugh over this! Did you hear him squeal? No one'd even touched him an' he squealed like a pig bein' killed. . . . Threw all his things away, too. Let's see if we can find any."

An exhaustive hunt revealed the cigarette-case and the note-book. Further down the road Ginger found the wrist watch that had been the final offering of the fleeing figure. . . . They discussed the ethics of the case in lowered voices.

"Well, he threw 'em away," said William. "'Tisn't even as if he'd lost 'em an' we'd found 'em. He *threw* 'em away. Well, I bet that's same as *givin'* 'em, by lor. I *bet* it's the same as if he'd *given* 'em us. An' anyway we don't know who he is, so we can't take 'em back. An' if we left 'em here someone else'd only find 'em an' keep 'em. 'Sides, there's a lor 'Finding's keepin' ' so it mus' be all right. I bet we're axshully *s'posed* to keep 'em by lor."

Having thus settled the question to their entire satisfaction, they proceeded to divide the spoil. For no particular reason William wanted the cigarette-case. He'd always wanted a cigarette-case. It was a grown-up sort of thing to have, and he could keep things in it. He wasn't quite sure yet what he could keep in it, but he was quite sure that he could keep things in it. Ginger was equally anxious to possess the wrist watch, and Henry was quite willing to be put off with the note-book.

"I bet he was a German spy," said Henry. "I *bet* he was. That was why he ran off like that. Well, he *couldn't*'ve been scared of ole Harry Dare. How *could* he—a big man like that? An' he didn't mean to throw away the note-book. He dropped it by mistake. I bet he did. . . . An' I bet I find a lot of German spy stuff in it. I'm goin' to send it up to the King if I do, an' I bet he'll give me a reward for helpin' win the war. . . ."

It was the next afternoon. Claude Brading was again having tea with Philippa. He was feeling quite happy to-day, because the chauffeur was to call for him and take him home, and the nervous wear and tear of yesterday's journey would be avoided. He had given considerable thought to yesterday's journey. Back in his well-lighted bedroom, he had realised that the incident did not tally with the stories of his bravery that he had broadcast so recently. Actually he would have liked to ignore the whole thing, but unfortunately that was impossible, for the cigarette-case that he had thrust into the unknown's hands had been given him last month as a birthday present by Philippa, and she would at once notice its disappearance. She had sulked on several occasions because he had forgotten to bring it with him and had produced instead a paper packet of cigarettes. "Of course," she had said coldly, "if you don't like it . . ." and it had taken him quite a long time to convince her that he did. . . . He must find some explanation of its disappearance. Then suddenly it occurred to him that the whole thing might be turned to his advantage. A little "embroidery" was all that was needed. . . .

He was rather annoyed to find Robert there, firmly established in the Pomeroy drawing-room, but the

obvious relief with which Philippa greeted him showed
that she was finding Robert as dull as ever.

"An extraordinary thing happened to me last night,"
he said with an airy smile as he took his tea cup. "I mean
extraordinary when you remember what we were talking
about yesterday."

"What were we talking about?" said Philippa.

"Hold-ups and robberies during the black-out,"
Claude reminded her.

"Oh yes—I remember."

"Well, the extraordinary thing is," said Claude, still
with the airy smile, "that I was attacked myself on my
way home."

The announcement caused a sensation that satisfied
even Claude.

"Oh *Claude*!" said Philippa, clasping her hands in
flattering solicitude.

Robert was interested despite himself.

"I say!" he said. "Where?"

"I'm afraid I'm not too good at geography in a black-
out," said Claude. "All I can tell you is that it happened
somewhere between here and my own home. It was a
gang."

Again the effect was flattering.

"A gang?" said Philippa, and:

"Good Lord!" said Robert.

"Oh, yes," said Claude easily. "These things aren't
as a rule done by local men. Gangs of ruffians go from
place to place attacking pedestrians on the road in the
black-out. Most of them are professional boxers and
come from as far afield as London, I believe. There were
four or five men in the gang that attacked me."

Again Philippa's gasp of horror was music in his ear.

"Of course, if I hadn't been a bit of a boxer myself,"

went on Claude modestly, "well—I mightn't be here to tell the tale. They were a pretty desperate lot."

"What did they do?" said Robert.

"What did they do?" repeated Claude, with a smile. "They just set about me, that's what they did. They kept me pretty busy, I can tell you. By the time I'd got the fourth one down on the ground the first one was getting up. I managed to stun two of them, and that only left me two to deal with and I made short work of them."

"Oh, Claude!" said Philippa rapturously.

Robert was looking at him with what Claude inwardly termed a nasty look. Green with jealousy, of course, thought Claude. *He'd* never have the pluck to put up a fight against four professional boxing thugs, for by now Claude almost believed his own story.

"Four of them, did you say?" said Robert, and added, "you're very little marked for a fight like that."

"Marked?" said Claude, with a short laugh. "My dear fellow, I'm a fighter of some experience. I've learnt how to keep an opponent off. No, any 'marking' will be found among my attackers. In fact I think that at least two of them will be in a pretty bad way this afternoon."

"What a good thing it ended all right, anyway," said Philippa. "I hope you've told the police."

"Well," hesitated Claude, "I—I shall have to do that, I suppose, because unfortunately, though I beat the blighters off, I managed to lose something I prize very much."

"How was that?" said Robert, still with the nasty look on his face.

Claude ignored him and continued his explanation to Philippa.

"There was a fifth man that I didn't see till the end. He was evidently a professional pickpocket and rifled my pockets, etc., while I was engaged in the fight. I noticed him running off with the others when they'd had enough, but it wasn't till some time after that I realised he'd picked my pockets. He took my watch (which happened to be in my pocket) my note-book and my money, but I don't mind that. What I do mind," here he fixed his eyes soulfully on Philippa, "is that the wretch took the cigarette-case you gave me and that I prize more than all my other possessions put together."

"Oh, well," said Philippa generously, "you couldn't help it. I do see that you couldn't help it. Perhaps the police will get it back for you. I do hope they will because—well, after all, it *means* something to you, doesn't it?"

"It means everything to me," said Claude, in a deep earnest voice.

"Odd that you haven't even got a black eye," put in Robert.

"Why?" said Claude, in a tone of light amusement. "I've no doubt that you'd have had two black eyes *and* a broken nose in my place, but I happen to have my own technique. However," modestly, "I've done quite enough talking about myself. Let's talk of something else. . . ."

So he proceeded to talk about the holiday he had spent abroad last summer and how amusing the "natives" had been and how deeply they had been impressed by him. It was just as he was describing how he had got the better of a taxi man who was trying to charge him more than the legal fare that William and Ginger entered. William had not forgotten the excellent tea he had had here yesterday, nor the way Mr. Brading had pressed him to have second and third helpings of everything, nor the kind invitation to come again and bring a friend. He had taken the invitation at its face value and, quite simply, he had come again and brought a friend. The friend wore an enormous wrist watch of severely masculine design, several times too large for him, but for the moment this was hidden from view by the sleeve of a new coat, which had been chosen by his mother with a view to "allowing for growth".

Claude remembered how he had amused Philippa yesterday by baiting William, so he continued the process, pressing William to have more cake, asking him what he used for his hair, complimenting him on his table manners, as the pattern of the carpet round his feet gradually vanished under a cloud of cake crumbs. William, who was unaccustomed to this particular brand of sarcasm, continued to enjoy the party. It was the best chocolate cake he'd ever tasted, Mr. Brading was showering compliments upon him (and William appreciated a compliment as much as anyone else), and there was a general atmosphere of mirth and amiability. Miss Pomeroy kept roaring with laughter—for no particular reason that William could see, but it helped to make things jolly, and William liked things to be jolly. True, Robert sat glowering at him furiously, but William was used to Robert's glowering at him furiously. Whenever they met at anyone's house, Robert sat like that and glowered at him furiously. Robert, of course, liked to be alone with Miss Pomeroy, but, anyway, Mr. Brading was there, and Miss Pomeroy was quite obviously enjoying his, William's, company.

"What about the friend?" Mr. Brading was saying. "Can I tempt his appetite with just a small chocolate biscuit? What he's eaten will surely hardly sustain him till supper time."

Ginger stretched out his hand for the biscuit, and—

the grin dropped from Claude's face like something being wiped off a slate. For the movement had brought up the cuff of his coat and revealed the large masculine wrist watch that Claude had thrown away the evening before. There was no mistaking it. As a mother knows her child, so a young man knows his wrist watch. There was even the slight crack across the glass face that Claude was always meaning to get repaired. . . . He fell suddenly silent, ceasing to fling his shafts of wit at the visitors. He didn't want to ask Ginger how he'd got it till he knew how he *had* got it. The thought that someone besides himself knew the truth of the "attack" and "theft" sent hot and cold shivers all over him. . . .

"Tell these children about those men who attacked you last night, Claude," said Philippa suddenly. "I'm sure it would thrill them."

"Well—er," said Claude, passing a finger round the top of his collar, "well—er—I'm quite sure you're tired of the story."

His eyes were fixed like those of a fascinated rabbit on the wrist watch that was still partly visible beneath Ginger's cuff.

"I'm not," said Philippa. "I'd love to hear it again. Wouldn't you, Robert?"

Robert grunted and pulled out a packet of cigarettes. He opened them, handed them to Claude, and took one himself.

"Can I have the card, please?" said William, his mouth full of orange cake.

Robert set his teeth. That awful kid letting him down all over the place, as usual. Turning up without being asked, eating like a cannibal, strewing crumbs right and left, talking with his mouth full, turning himself and the whole family (as it seemed to the outraged Robert) into an Aunt Sally for that fool Brading to take pot shots at—and now having the nerve to ask for a cigarette card. He was putting the packet back into his pocket without even looking at him, when Philippa said sweetly:

"Let him have it, Robert."

Mentally, Robert added to his score against William the fact that he had made him appear in Philippa's eyes the sort of man who is unkind to his little brother. Without a word, still scowling furiously, he handed the cigarette card to William. Without a word, but with a tremendous flourish, William brought a cigarette-case out of his pocket. After much thought he had decided to use his new treasure as a receptacle for cigarette cards. It would give him plenty of opportunities to display it and he enjoyed displaying it. . . .

"This is where I keep 'em," he began to explain with an air of modest pride, but he was interrupted by a scream from Philippa, who snatched the case out of his hand, scattering his cigarette cards far and wide.

"It's your case," she said to Claude, with a hysterical gasp in her voice. "The one that was stolen."

"Well, it's like it," said Claude, catching at a straw, "but a lot of these things are turned out just the same."

Philippa was examining the inside of the case.

"But it's got your initials in. . . . It must be."

"Well—er—yes, it must be," said Claude, letting the straw go (he'd forgotten the initials for the moment). "Er—yes, it must be."

"Where did you find it?" said Philippa to William. "Where on *earth* did you find it?"

"Where did you find it?" mumbled Claude, his cheeks pale, his eyes glassy with apprehension.

"Yes, where did you find it?" said Robert sternly.

(Gosh! was there no end to the humiliations that wretched kid brought on one?)

"I was goin' to tell you that," said William, selecting another piece of cake and taking a large bite. "I was jus' goin'——" A look of horror stole over his face. "Gosh! Seed! I didn't know it was seed when I took it." The look of horror changed to agony as he manfully swallowed the mouthful. "I can't think why people *make* it, seed cake. *Seeds* in *cake*! It's cracked. Jus' a waste of seeds an'

"I WAS JUS' GOIN' TO TELL YOU," REPEATED WILLIAM.

cake. You can't use the seeds for sowin' 'cause of the cake an' you can't use the cake for eatin' 'cause of the seeds. I think——"

"Where—did—you—get—that—cigarette—case?" said Robert through clenched teeth.

"I was jus' goin' to tell you," repeated William, "when I took that awful seed cake. I say," to Philippa, "can I have another piece of chocolate cake, please—to take the taste away? Thanks. It's a funny thing but once

**"WHERE—DID—YOU—GET—THAT—CIGARETTE—CASE?" SAID
ROBERT THROUGH CLENCHED TEETH.**

I've had a bit of seed cake I go on tastin' an' tastin' it till I've had another sort of cake to take the taste away. An' choc'late——"

"WHERE——" began Robert again furiously.

"Oh yes," interrupted William harshly, "I remember. Well, I was goin' to tell you but that seed cake made me forget all about it. You'd hardly b'lieve I could still taste it, would you, 'spite of the chocolate cake——"

Claude, tortured beyond endurance, made a little moaning sound that he turned hastily into a cough.

"Well, it was this way," said William, highly flattered by the interest the whole company was showing in his recital, his voice muffled by a mouthful of chocolate cake. "It was jolly funny an' I bet it'd make you laugh." He turned his ingenuous admiring gaze on to the quaking Claude. "That's what I said to Ginger afterwards. I said to Ginger, 'It'd make Mr. Brading laugh all right.' That was partly why I came round this afternoon 'cause I thought you'd be here an' it'd make you laugh. . . . Well, you see, this man——"

"What man?" snapped Robert, while Claude made the little moaning sound again and turned it into another cough.

"Well, we were out after the black-out—me an' Ginger an' Henry—an' this man was goin' down the road an' Harry Dare came out of the wood and sort of banged into him by mistake, an' the man said, 'Don't, don't, I'll give you everything I've got,' an' he took everythin' out of his pocket and pushed it at Harry Dare and then he ran off an' he threw his watch down the road while he was runnin' off, an' said, 'Take it, take it' though Harry Dare hadn't said a word. An' Harry Dare threw the things down 'cause I s'pose he didn't want 'em 'cept three ten-shilling notes what he put in his pocket an' went off, so Ginger an' Henry an' me picked up the things. Ginger got the wrist watch. Show 'em your wrist watch, Ginger."

Ginger proudly extended his wrist, and Claude, green about the gills, but wearing a fixed and glassy smile, pulled down his sleeve so that the absence of his own watch should not be noticed. Philippa stared at the watch, her eyes growing wider and wider, her mouth grimmer. She, too, recognised the little crack across the glass face. She had, in fact, been there when it was made. Claude had been demonstrating the technique of the knock-out blow that always stunned his assailant, and his watch had come in contact with a chair back.

"An' I took the case," went on William garrulously, quite unmoved by the tension around him, "'cause I thought it would do to keep things in. Well, two people'd thrown them away, so we thought we could take 'em, all right. The man couldn't 've wanted 'em or he wouldn't 've thrown 'em at Harry Dare. An' Harry Dare couldn't 've wanted 'em or he wouldn't 've thrown 'em away. So I bet it's all right us takin' 'em. Henry took the note-book 'cause he thought this man might be a German spy. There's a lot of stuff in it that sounds all right, but Henry thinks it's a code. It says things like, 'Skating rink at Hadley with P.', an' 'Pictures at Hadley with P.', an' 'Bought P. a crocodile skin handbag for birthday present'." (Claude moaned again and Philippa gasped.) "But Henry's sure it's a code. He's workin' it out but he's not made anythin' fit in yet." He chuckled and looked at Claude. "Corks! You'd 've laughed all right, Mr. Brading. I'd jus' been tellin' Ginger an' Henry about all those men you'd fought an' rescued an' such like, an' to see this man—he was as big as you, too—yell out an' say, 'Don't, don't,' soon as he saw

Harry Dare, when Harry hadn't even touched him, and throw all his stuff at him—well, it's jolly funny, if you know Harry Dare."

They all knew Harry Dare—undersized, weakly, timorous, despite his skill at poaching.

There was a long, long silence. During that long silence it struck William for the first time that something was wrong. Mr. Brading looked queer, Miss Pomeroy looked queer, Robert looked queer. It was Claude who broke the long silence.

"Of course, it's quite obvious what happened," he said in a curious high-pitched bleating voice. "Quite obvious. One of those men who attacked and robbed me was making off with the booty when he ran into this Harry Dare chap and—and—and—well, and thought the fellow was going to attack him and so—well, handed the stuff on to him and made off. Probably he *did* attack him, and these boys just didn't see."

"No, he didn't attack him," said William. "Ole Harry Dare was jus' as scared as the other man. He jus' put up his stick to keep him off, that was all. But I say," earnestly, "do tell us about those four men what attacked you. I'd jolly well like to hear about that."

"I'm sure you would," said Philippa icily, "and no doubt Mr. Brading will tell you about it some time. . . . It makes an excellent tale. Meantime you'd better give him back his property."

Reluctantly they handed Claude his cigarette-case and watch. He pocketed them, still wearing a glassy smile.

"T-t-t-f-thanks," he stammered. "I'll get in touch with the police at once."

"I shouldn't trouble to do that," said Philippa bitterly. "I hardly think the police could help in this particular case."

"Perhaps not," said Claude with a ghastly attempt at joviality. "They're not a very bright lot round here, are they?"

"How many men did you say set on you?" said William admiringly. "Four, did you say? Gosh! I bet you beat 'em off all right."

Nobody spoke. William stared at them mystified. He realised that something had gone wrong with the party, but he couldn't think what it was. Had he made too many crumbs, he wondered, and stooped surreptitiously to pick a few up.

"Well," said Claude, rising and speaking with an unconvincing imitation of his usual airy manner. "I'd better be getting . . ." He turned to Philippa. "Don't forget that you're going with me to the Bruces' dance to-night."

Philippa gave him a look compared with which a glacier would have seemed tropical.

"I don't think so," she said. "You see, there's the question of the black-out, and I can't run as fast as you." She turned a shatteringly sweet smile on to Robert. "Will you take me to the Bruces' dance, Robert?"

William stared at them all in amazement. . . .

*   *   *

William trudged upstairs to bed. Robert, in a state of fatuous imbecility, had gone off to the Bruces' dance with Philippa. All very well for him, thought William morosely. For William the day had been a depressing one. Not only had he had to give up a cigarette-case that he had come to look on as his own property, but he had learnt that yet another hero had feet of clay. It was Mr. Brading who had turned to flee from Harry Dare. Therefore Mr. Brading could not have played the central part in those thrilling dramas that had so fired William's imagination. . . . Worst of all, he seemed as far off the tin hat as ever. Disillusioned and depressed, he dragged the toes of his shoes heavily on each step as he went upstairs.

"William, do stop wearing out the carpets like that," said Mrs. Brown, coming into the hall.

William gave a hollow laugh and began lifting his feet unduly high on to each step.

"Oh, by the way," said Mrs. Brown, "Robert said he'd put something in your bedroom for you."

"Huh!" said William. "I've prob'ly got it. I've never known Robert give me a cigarette card I've not got. I s'pose it *is* a cigarette card."

"He didn't say what it was," said Mrs. Brown, going back into the drawing-room.

"*Bet* it's one I've got," said William.

He went into his bedroom.

Immediately life became rapturous, ecstatic, flooded with *couleur de rose*.

For there on his bed lay a magnificent new tin hat.

Chapter 8

William Gets his Own Back

The news that Farmer Jenks's Four Acre meadow had once more been let to campers spread quickly among the junior inhabitants of the village. It had been empty since the departure of the campers with whom Mr. Brown's cousin from Africa had apparently dealt so summarily, and the memory made the Outlaws more than usually interested in the newcomers. On the evening of their arrival William and Ginger went to the meadow to investigate matters, but all they could see was a confused crowd of boys unpacking tents and equipment under the charge of a pallid young man in spectacles, whose costume of open shirt and shorts revealed a startlingly large Adam's apple in a very thin neck and a pair of regrettably knock knees. William, who had been raised a bit above himself by his experience with the previous campers, hurled a few experimental insults over the hedge. At first the campers ignored him, but finally a gorilla-like youth, with red hair and enormous arms, came towards the hedge in such a threatening manner that William and Ginger fled precipitately without having obtained any information about their new neighbours. The next few days, however, furnished them with a good deal. The elder portion consisted of a set of boys of school-leaving age, who at home formed a gang, called the Red Heads, from their leader's blazing poll. They roamed the streets, fought with rival gangs, and frequently got into trouble with the police. The man in charge, who had undertaken that unenviable position reluctantly and only because the friend who originally undertook it got 'flu at the last minute, had a wholesome awe of them and ignored them as far as possible. He had acquaintances in the neighbourhood and spent a good deal of time going out to lunch and tea, taking with him the younger and more presentable of the boys, and, wisely perhaps, leaving the Red Heads to their own devices. They wandered down the lanes in search of rival gangs to fight—and found the Outlaws. They recognised William and Ginger as the boys who had hurled insults over the hedge the first evening and set about them with joyful battle cries. They set about them to some purpose, too, and it was a mauled and mangled band that finally escaped to flee for safety to the old barn.

"Gosh!" panted William. "I feel's if they've broke every bone I've got."

"It wasn't fair," said Ginger, indignantly. "They're older than us."

"An' there's more of 'em," said Douglas.

"I say," said Henry suddenly. "I'd like 'em to smash up Hubert Lane's gang."

They saw them smash up Hubert Lane's gang the next day. It was a heartening sight (Hubert's yells could be heard as far away as Marleigh) but, in spite of that, it did not altogether restore the spirits of the Outlaws. For, though the defeat of the Hubert Laneites had been ignominious, their own had been only a little less so.

"I bet that ole Hubert'll be black an' blue," said Ginger.

"I'm still black an' blue myself," admitted William.

"I saw Bertie Franks's nose bleedin'," said Henry.

"Mine was bleedin', too," said Douglas.

"An' they'll do it again every time any of us go out," predicted Ginger gloomily.

It was Henry who, somewhat tentatively, voiced the most obvious solution of the problem.

"If we joined up with the Hubert Laneites we'd all have more chance," he said.

They considered this unprecedented proposal without enthusiasm. In ordinary circumstances it would have been outrageous, but the circumstances were not ordinary. Some drastic step must be taken, or the Outlaws would find themselves cut off indefinitely from their favourite haunts.

"If it wasn't for that girl——" said William.

"That girl" was Queenie Lane—a cousin of Hubert's who was staying with the Lanes and had constituted herself a member of Hubert's gang. She was indeed now to all practical purposes the leader, for she was possessed of an almost super-human degree of determination, and it would have taken a more courageous boy than Hubert to stand up to her. She had closely cropped hair, a ferocious stare and an aggressive manner, and William hated her with a peculiar intensity.

"We can squash *her*, all right," said Ginger.

"No, we can't," said William. "No one can squash her. Not that sort of a girl. I've tried. I'm jolly well not goin' to join up with them if *she's* goin' to be in it. Queenie!" he ejaculated with disgust. "It jolly well suits her all right. An' that ole Hubert ought to be called Kingie. They're a couple of softies."

"She's not a softie," said Ginger thoughtfully, remembering various exhibitions of the lady's temper that he had been privileged to witness.

"Yes, she is," said William scornfully. "Carryin' on an' making scenes! Jus' like a girl. Anyway I'm not goin' to join up with *her*. I'd rather be licked by the Red Heads."

"Well, let's go'n' ask him," suggested Henry. "It can't do any harm to go'n' ask him."

Cautiously and by a devious route, scanning the horizon anxiously for enemies, they made their way to Hubert's house. Hubert was at the gate, also scanning the horizon anxiously for enemies. By him stood Queenie and behind him hovered his gang.

"Jus' seein' if it looked like rain," said Hubert casually. "We—we're goin' out but we thought we'd see if it looked like rain first."

Ordinarily the Outlaws would have jeered at this flimsy excuse for cowardice, but they felt a certain bond of sympathy with the Hubert Laneites just now, and forbore to comment on it.

"Can we come in for a minute?" said William, in a brusque business-like voice. His face wore a fixed and resolute expression, the expression of one who wants to get through an unpleasant business as quickly as possible.

Silently Hubert Lane opened the gate. Silently the Outlaws trooped in. Queenie fixed him with a fish-like stare. William had freely voiced his dislike of girls in general and herself in particular, and she was not a girl to forget an insult. William tried not to look at her. She was built on stalwart lines, and she wore a pair of green linen shorts that she had out-grown but that her mother had said would do at a pinch for another summer. "At a pinch" expressed it well. . . . William found that he disliked her even more than he had thought he did.

"It's about those Red Heads," he began.

"Yes?" said Hubert nervously.

He always felt a little apprehensive in the presence of the Outlaws and was assuring himself that if they started any rough business his mother was indoors and within call.

"They jolly well knocked you about the other day, didn't they?" said William, "so we thought," assuming an air of aloof generosity, "p'raps you'd like us to help you nex' time. Go about with you an' so on."

"They knocked you about, too," put in Bertie Franks.

Queenie continued to fix William with the fish-like stare and say nothing.

"Oh, that was nothin'," said William airily. "Jus' a little wrestlin' match, that was all. But—well, we thought they *might* knock us about, same as they knocked you, an' that if we joined up together. . . ."

"Oo yes. . . ." said Hubert eagerly. "That'd be jolly fine."

"But we don't want girls," said William firmly. "If we join up with you, there's not gotter be any girls in it."

Hubert glanced apprehensively at Queenie. She continued to fix William with a stare that now was suggestive of an outraged cod.

"Well . . ." he began.

Queenie spoke for the first time.

"If Hubert's joinin' up with you, I'm joinin' up with you," she said in her deep slow voice. "I'm part of your gang, aren't I, Hubert?"

"Er—yes," agreed Hubert nervously.

"Well, then," said Queenie, "if the gang joins up, I

join up.. An', if I don't join up, the gang doesn't join up. See?"

"I've jus' told you, haven't I," said William sternly, "that I don't want girls?"

"IF HUBERT'S JOININ' UP WITH YOU, I'M JOININ' UP WITH YOU," SAID QUEENIE IN HER DEEP SLOW VOICE.

Queenie, hands on hips, took a step forward, confronting him aggressively. She tried to set her jaw but her jaw was slightly underhung so that two large front teeth always protruded. They gave her the appearance of a massive and very ferocious rabbit.

"An' why don't you want girls?" she said grimly.

"'Cause they're rotten ole cissies," said William

scornfully. "Rotten ole cissies, that's what they are. They're cowardy custards an' they've got no sense an' they spoil everythin' they join in at. I'd sooner not have a gang at all than have a rotten ole girl in it."

"I'VE JUS' TOLD YOU, HAVEN'T I?" SAID WILLIAM STERNLY, "THAT I DON'T WANT GIRLS?"

Queenie's usually putty-coloured face turned a bright red. Hubert looked helplessly from one to the other.

"You're a rotten ole cowardy custard yourself," said Queenie, advancing her face to an inch or two of William's, "an' you're the ugliest boy I ever saw an' I hate you an'——"

"I don't care if you do," said William. "I'd sooner

rotten ole girls hated me. An' take your ole face off me. . . ."

Unable any longer to endure the close proximity of Queenie's face and unwilling to give the appearance of retreat by stepping back from it, William put out a hand and unceremoniously pushed it away. Taken by surprise, Queenie lost her balance and fell on to the gravel. She sat there for a moment, too enraged to breathe, then let forth a resounding bellow of pain and rage.

William ignored her, turning to Hubert.

"'Bout this joinin' up," he began, but Hubert's eyes were fixed fearfully on the redoubtable Queenie.

"I can't if she won't," he explained in an undertone. "You'd better go. She's in an awful bait. . . ."

"I'm not frightened of any rotten ole girl," said William, but he realised that the situation was not a propitious one for carrying on delicate negotiations, and, summoning his band, set off homewards.

"Rotten ole girls," he grumbled as they went. "Didn't I say they were always making fusses, an' spoilin' things? I wish I'd knocked her ole face right off. I would of done, too, if she'd kept it there much longer. . . ."

"I'm sorry we couldn't join up with his gang," said Ginger regretfully. "We'll get knocked about again by those Red Heads."

"I'd rather be knocked about by Red Heads," persisted William, "than join up with a rotten ole girl!"

"So would we," agreed the others heartily.

But the next day made them change their minds. The Red Heads lay in wait for them and inflicted an even more crushing defeat than any of their former ones. Queenie, too, was induced to change her mind, for the Red Heads also waylaid the Hubert Laneites and pushed

Queenie into a ditch, from which she emerged coated with mud from head to foot.

The next day Hubert, accompanied by Bertie Franks, approached the Outlaws. Queenie hovered in the background, still fixing William with that unblinking hostile stare.

"I say," said Hubert, "about this joinin' up. . . ."

"Told you I didn't want girls," said William, but without the firmness he had displayed on the previous occasion. "Rotten ole cissies!"

Queenie said nothing. Her hostile stare did not falter.

"Yes, but——" began Hubert and left the sentence unfinished.

William, of course, saw the point that Hubert had tactfully refrained from putting into words. Better a girl in the gang than these continual defeats at the hands of their enemies.

"Very well," he said, after a pause, "but I've gotter be the head of it."

"That's all right," agreed Hubert eagerly (for Hubert had no desire at all to lead his forces or anyone else's into danger). He turned pacifically to Queenie: "That'll be all right, won't it, Queenie?"

"Yes," said Queenie slowly and without removing her fixed stare from William's face. "Yes, that'll be all right."

"An' you've all gotter do just what I tell you," said William.

"Yes, we will, won't we, Queenie?" agreed Hubert.

"Oh, yes, we will," said Queenie.

William took for granted that Queenie had accepted him unquestioningly as her leader. A wiser boy would have known better. . . .

William proceeded to lay his plans. The Red Heads

now counted on the hostility of the Outlaws and Hubert Laneites to each other. It was a shock to them, therefore, the next day, when they attacked the Hubert Laneites in the road near the camp, to be attacked in their turn by the Outlaws, who sprang out of ambush in defence of their allies. The combination was too much for the Red Heads. In the short sharp fight that followed they were completely routed. Even Hubert, heartened by their superiority in numbers, fought quite creditably, and Queenie's method of selecting such Red Heads as were already engaged with an opponent and attacking them from behind with a pointed stick, contributed in no small measure to the victory. So accustomed had the Outlaws and Hubert Laneites become to defeat in the last few days that when they saw the Red Heads turn to flee they stood for a moment irresolute, not quite knowing what to do. William assumed his position as leader.

"Come on," he shouted. "After 'em, quick!"

They rallied their forces to pursue the fleeing foe—more because the pursuit of a fleeing foe is the right thing after a successful engagement than because they had the faintest idea what to do with any fleeing foe they might capture. They were indeed more disconcerted than gratified when a Red Head tripped over a large stone in the lane and lay there at their mercy. They surrounded him, watching him apprehensively as he scrambled to his feet. Once more William took command of the situation.

"Get hold of him," he said sternly. "Take him prisoner."

Tentatively, cautiously, the Outlaws laid hold of the Red Head, while the Hubert Laneites stood in the background ready for instant flight should he prove too much for them. But the Red Head was, as it happened, the most timorous of the gang, one who had been only recently admitted to it—more for the reason that he possessed an entire cricket set than for any particularly warlike qualities. He had, moreover, had his nose bashed by William and his head cracked open (as it seemed to him) by Ginger, and he looked on the Outlaws as a set of ferocious savages from whom the ordinary amenities of civilised warfare could not be expected. He was an under-sized youth, with a rat-like nose and a receding chin, and he wore a violent green and red check shirt with his very yellow khaki shorts. He scrambled to his knees.

"'Ere," he pleaded. "'Ere, I 'aven't done yer no 'arm, 'ave I? I din't want to fight yer. I din't—I——"

"Stick 'em up," said William, encouraged by his enemy's timidity.

The captive stuck 'em up.

Then came a short silence, during which the Outlaws again wondered helplessly what to do with him. The situation was unprecedented. They'd never taken a prisoner before. Again it was William, as leader, who gave the necessary orders.

"To the ole barn!" he ordered, in his best dictator manner. "Quick march!"

Outlaws and Hubert Laneites set off to the old barn, the prisoner in their midst. Having arrived at the old barn, William left the Red Head there under an ample guard and withdrew a short distance with Ginger and Hubert to discuss the situation.

"Well, what're we goin' to *do* with him?" demanded Ginger.

William had a sudden inspiration.

"We'll *question* him," he said. "That's what they do with prisoners. They *question* 'em."

"TO THE OLE BARN!" ORDERED WILLIAM, IN HIS BEST
DICTATOR MANNER. "QUICK MARCH!"

"What about?" demanded Hubert.

"About their mil'tary secrets, of course," said
William impatiently.

"S'pose they've not got any?"

"Of *course* they've got mil'tary secrets," said
William. "All enemies've got mil'tary secrets."

"We oughter *torcher* him," said Queenie, who had
suddenly appeared in their midst.

William scowled at her.

"Nobody asked *you* to say anythin'," he said crushingly.

"An' no one asked *you* to, either," countered Queenie.

William ignored this and, turning his shoulder on her to exclude her from the conference of leaders, went on:

"That's what they do in all the tales I've read. They question 'em an' get their mil'tary secrets out of 'em."

"In all the tales I've read they *torcher* 'em," said Queenie, who by some acrobatic feat had again taken her place in the centre of the group. "They get their mil'tary secrets out of 'em by *torcher*."

"*You!*" said William contemptuously. "I bet you've never read anythin' but Tiny Tots."

Queenie swallowed hard.

"Oh, haven't I?" she said furiously. "Oh——"

Rage deprived her of further speech.

William took advantage of her temporary eclipse to return to the old barn accompanied by Ginger and Hubert. The prisoner had ensconced himself comfortably on a packing case and was engaged in cracking and eating nuts, of which he evidently had a plentiful supply in the pockets of his khaki shorts. His captors stood around watching him uncertainly. They would have liked to ask him for a nut but were doubtful how far the etiquette of the situation allowed such overtures. William took up his position in front of him, covering his slight uncertainty as to correct procedure by an exaggeratedly ferocious manner.

"Now you've gotter give us your mil'tary secrets," he said sternly.

The Red Head, who was of somewhat low intelligence, looked at him doubtfully, then took a small handful of nuts out of his pocket and held them out to William.

"A'right," he said, "but they're not what you said. They're monkey nuts."

William, who had a weakness for monkey nuts, looked at them wistfully then, remembering the dignity of his position, waved them loftily aside.

"I don't mean that," he said. "I mean——" He paused uncertainly. "I mean, what're you goin' to do?"

The Red Head considered the question.

"I'm goin' to have my tea," he said, "soon as I get back to camp."

"Pull his teeth out," said Queenie, appearing suddenly at William's elbow.

William ignored her.

"No, I don't mean that," he said. "I mean—I mean—well, what're the others goin' to do?"

"Have their tea too," said the Red Head simply.

He was obviously anxious to give William all the information in his possession.

"Stick pins into him," said Queenie.

"Shut up," said William irritably. Then to the Red Head: "No, I din't mean that. I meant what—what *plans* have you got?"

"Plans?" said the Red Head mystified.

"Yes—what're you goin' to do?"

"Have my tea," said the Red Head again patiently.

"Pull his hair," said Queenie.

"Shut *up*," snapped William. "Now listen," to the Red Head. "We'll let you go if you'll tell us what—well," feebly, "what you're all *plannin'* to do. You know. When you're goin' to *attack* us an'—an' that sort of thing."

"Oh, I don't know," said the Red Head casually. "I

don't know nothin' about that." He spat out some monkey nut shells. "I jus' do what they tell me, that's all I do. I gotter cricket set," he ended proudly.

"Told you he wouldn't tell you anything till you'd *torchered* him," said Queenie vehemently.

"I have tol' you somethin'," said the Red Head indignantly. "I've tol' you I've gotter cricket set. I'm goin' to play with it when I've had my tea."

William looked at him helplessly. They seemed to be going round and round in a circle and always coming back to the Red Head's tea. And that reminded William that he, too, was hungry and that it was past his tea time. There didn't seem much point in continuing the somewhat ineffectual examination of the prisoner.

"Well," he said lamely, "p'raps we'd better all go now. . . ."

"You're not goin' to let *him* go, are you?" demanded Queenie indignantly, pointing to the prisoner.

"Well, why not?" said William. "He can't tell us anythin'. He doesn't seem to *know* anythin'. 'Sides, I want my tea, too."

"Well, if you're goin' to have your tea," said Queenie, "you ought to keep him here an' leave someone to guard him."

"We all want our tea," said William simply. "No one wants to stay an' guard him."

"I will," offered Queenie. "I'll stay an' guard him. Then when you come back we can have a sort of tri'l of him."

"All right," said William, yielding somewhat reluctantly. It certainly seemed a little feeble just to let the prisoner go. . . . Moreover, the Red Head, though undersized, was obviously more than a match for Queenie, and he rather hoped that she would make herself so objectionable as a jailer that she would at last get what had long been coming to her.

"All right," he said. "Come on," to the others. "We'll go now, and"—sternly to Queenie—"mind you don't let him go."

Queenie stood at the door of the old barn watching him out of sight, and amusing herself by making hostile grimaces at his unconscious back. Then she joined her prisoner inside the barn. The idea of somehow getting even with William had been vaguely in her mind when she made the suggestion of guarding him, but she had as yet formed no definite plan. She must just see how things went. . . .

The prisoner was cracking his last nut.

"Hello," she said amicably.

He looked up at her.

"Hello," he replied indifferently. He stood up. "Well, I'll be gettin' back to camp to tea now. Wasted a lot o' time comin' 'ere. Wanter play with my cricket set. I lost the ball this mornin' an' I wanter find it."

"Wait a bit," said Queenie. "I'm goin' back through the village, too, an' if you'll come with me I'll buy some more monkey nuts an' give you half."

"Reelly?" he said incredulously.

She nodded.

"Yes. Honest. Go on. Tell me what you're goin' to do to-morrow."

"To-morrow?" said the Red Head vaguely. "I dunno."

"I bet you do," said Queenie. "See here. I'll give you *all* the monkey nuts if you'll tell me."

He looked at her craftily.

"You'll tell those chaps an' they'll come an' stop us."

"I won't," promised Queenie. "Honest I won't. I promise. Cross my throat."

"You'll tell that boss of their gang—that mutt they call William."

Queenie's face grew rigid with fury at the thought of William.

"*That* boy?" she said. "Bossing our gang about as if he was Hitler or someone! They jolly well did what I told them before *he* came along. Bossing and ordering about! An' that old softie of a Hubert lettin' him!"

"Which is he?" said the Red Head. "The fat 'un?"

"Yes," said Queenie. "But he was all right before that ole boss of a William got hold of him. He did what I said then. That ole William! I'd like to see him *torchered*."

"Thought it was me you wanted torchered," said the Red Head mildly.

"Oh *no!*" said Queenie. "It was him I meant. It was *him* I wanted torchered, all right!" She lowered her voice persuasively. "See here. I'm on your side. I hate that ole boss of a William so's I'd be on anyone's side that wasn't his. I'll be one of your gang. A sort of secret member. I'll do anythin' you like."

The Red Head looked at her speculatively.

"You'll give me *all* the monkey nuts!" he stipulated.

"Yes," promised Queenie and continued wildly, throwing caution to the winds. "*An*' a bag of humbugs *an*' a lollypop an' a packet of sherbet. I'll spend all the money I was saving up for a bicycle. I'd got nearly three shillings an' I want a bicycle more'n anythin' else in the world so that shows I'm on your side. That ole William wants a bicycle, too, but he's not got any money at all, an' he's not likely to get any, so I bet I get one sooner than him even if I have to start savin' all over again.

Listen. I'll spend *all* the money I've got. I'll buy you another cricket ball. . . ."

The Red Head's small eyes gleamed greedily.

"Sure you won't split?" he said.

"Sure. Honest. Cross my throat," affirmed Queenie.

"Well," he lowered his voice confidentially, "we was goin' to rob that orchard top of the hill."

"Farmer Jenks's?"

"Yeah. That's him."

Queenie was silent for a moment, wondering how best to turn this piece of information to her own advantage. Suddenly her face lit up.

"You could lick these two gangs all right before they joined together, couldn't you?" she said.

"Yeah," said the Red Head. "Easy, we could."

"Well, listen," said Queenie.

He listened, and a smile spread slowly over his ratlike face as he heard the details of her plan.

*   *   *

William and the Outlaws returned after an ample tea to find Queenie sitting at the doorway of the old barn, nibbling grass.

"He's escaped," she informed them calmly. "I jus' turned my back a minute an' he escaped."

William was secretly much relieved at the escape of the prisoner, but it seemed to offer him a good opportunity for pointing out the general uselessness of girls and he took full advantage of it.

"Jus' like a girl," he said scornfully. "Can't even look after a prisoner without lettin' him escape. Fine sort of *guard* you are! Talk about *torcherin'* him till we're sick of listenin' to you an' then all you can do is to let him escape."

Queenie fixed him with her slow unblinking stare for a moment then began to nibble grass again.

"Can't do anythin' but let him escape," repeated William, somewhat disconcerted by her silence. "Talk about *torcherin'* him, then can't do anything but let him escape. Jus' like a girl, that! Jolly good at talkin', all right. Oh yes! Jolly good at *talkin'* about torcherin' people, but can't do anything but let 'em escape. Oh yes. Jolly good at——"

Demoralised by Queenie's basilisk stare, he lost the thread, such as it was, of his remarks, and let his voice trail away uncertainly.

Then Queenie spoke in her slow deep voice.

"I *did* torcher him. I got all his plans out of him."

"I bet you didn't," said William.

"I did."

"You didn't."

"I did."

"You didn't."

"I did."

"*How* did you?" challenged William, seeing that she was determined to keep it up as long as he did.

"I told him I'd pull all his teeth out if he didn't tell me what they were goin' to do to-morrow."

"You *couldn't've* pulled all his teeth out," objected William.

"I know," said Queenie, inventing glibly, "but I told him you'd gone to get a machine to do it with, an' that you were guardin' all the gates an' things out of the field so it wasn't any good tryin' to escape, so—well, so he told me his plans, an' then I pretended to show him a secret way to escape, so he went. . . ."

William stared at her in unwilling respect. He disliked her as much as ever, but he had to admit that she got things done. It never occurred to him to doubt the truth of her story.

"Well, what *were* his plans?" he demanded, making an effort to retain his expression of dispassionate aloofness.

"They're goin' to rob Farmer Jenks's orchard to-morrow afternoon," said Queenie.

"Oh," said William.

He tried to look like the head of a totalitarian state and, having kept up the pose till he felt it slipping from him without having been able to come to any decision, said carelessly: "Well, we can't stop 'em doin' that, can we? There's no lor against robbin' orchards, is there?"

"We can do the same as we did to-day," said Queenie. "We can have one gang on the road so's they'll attack 'em an' the other in ambush to jump out at 'em."

William considered.

"We can't do that two days runnin'," he said at last. "They'd suspect."

"No, they won't," said Queenie. "I told him we'd quarrelled, an' weren't joinin' up any more."

William stared at her, impressed despite himself by her Machiavellian cunning. Then he said:

"I bet he di'n't believe you."

"He did," persisted Queenie.

"I bet he di'n't. I bet he only told you they were robbin' the orchard to put you off the scent, 'cause reely they're goin' to do somethin' quite different. An' even if they were I bet they won't do it now they find he's told you."

"Yes they *will*," persisted Queenie. "He won't tell 'em he told me. He daren't. He said he daren't. . . . They won't know we know. 'Sides, even if they don't go,

it won't do any *harm*. We'll go there just in case they do.
An' I bet they will go. We'll have one gang out in the
road an' the other in hiding same as we did to-day. Then
we'll smash 'em up again, an' after that they'll be so
scared of us they won't ever attack any of us again, 'case
the others are in hiding. An' if they don't come we can
jus' go away. It won't do any *harm*."

William looked at her helplessly. Queen Elizabeth
must have been like this, he thought, and that woman
with the funny name who rode in a chariot and led the
ancient Britons against Nero or someone. William wor-
shipped supermen, but had never had much opinion of
super-women. He felt that this girl's master mind was
jeopardising his position as leader.

"All right," he said coldly. "All right. I was just goin'
to s'gest that. I'd thought of it right from the beginning.
I'll go'n' tell the others now."

"Yes, do," said Queenie, "an' I'll tell Hubert."

He walked away with as much dignity as he could
muster, aware that Queenie was still sitting there, fixing
that cold basilisk stare on his back.

Next she approached Hubert. Hubert was a slightly
more difficult proposition. For Hubert was nervous and
afraid of incurring the hostility of the Outlaws. He was,
however, secretly jealous of William's command over
the two gangs, and his dislike of the Outlaws was so
fundamental that no truce could be anything but a
temporary one. Queenie, who, to do her justice was no
fool, played cleverly on these feelings.

"The way he bosses us about!" she said. "Same as if
we were all *his* rotten ole gang. I dunno how you stand
it, Hubert. Treats you like mud, he does. Makes me
mad."

"Makes me mad, too," muttered Hubert sulkily,

"but it's better than bein' bashed about by those old Red Heads."

"The way he carries on!" continued Queenie. "You'd think he was one of those axle people. Bossin' people about! I bet when those Red Heads go back you'll find you've not got any of your gang left. He'll have pinched 'em all."

Hubert turned pale at this prospect. It was indeed not an unlikely one, for there was no doubt that many of his followers enjoyed fighting under a leader of William's spirit. Queenie pursued her advantage.

"*That's* what he's trying to do," she said, "get your gang off you."

"D-d-do you think so?" stammered Hubert, who alone knew at what expenditure of money on treats and presents and parties the allegiance of his gang was secured.

"I do more 'n think," said Queenie darkly. "I *know*. That's all he wanted right from the beginning. To get your gang off you. Then, when you're all alone without any gang, he'll set 'em all on you every time he meets you. Bet they'll finish up by *killing* you," she ended darkly.

Hubert's fat face quivered and crumpled. His mouth opened for a howl of desolation. But Queenie hastily interposed.

"You'll be all right if you do what I say. The Red Heads are going to rob the orchard, an' the Outlaws'll be in the road, an' we're going to pretend to go in hiding but really we'll go right away an' leave the rotten ole Outlaws to get set on. The Red Heads know about it. I fixed it all up with that one we took prisoner. They know we're not goin' to be there, an' they're goin' to bring everyone they can get hold of to smash up those rotten old Outlaws. An' they won't touch us 'cause I'm a secret member of their gang now."

A shadow passed over her face as she thought of the price at which she had purchased membership. The three shillings had made the bicycle belong to the world of possibility. Now it was removed out of sight.

Hubert's face, however, relaxed into a satisfied grin. The picture Queenie had painted was a pleasant one, and he dwelt upon it zestfully. Then it clouded over.

"What about the rest of the gang?" he said. "Will they want to?"

For, except for his lieutenant, Bertie Franks, his gang did not share their leader's dislike of William. In fact, as I have said before, they enjoyed being led by a leader of courage and enterprise.

"We won't tell 'em," said Queenie simply. "We'll jus' tell 'em it's off an' that we've heard the Red Heads aren't goin' there, after all. You can leave that part to me."

Sunshine again flooded Hubert's chubby countenance.

*   *   *

Everything was in train. The Outlaws were making their way towards the road that led to Farmer Jenks's orchard. The Hubert Laneites were taking up their position in a small belt of trees just out of sight of the road but within range of William's pre-arranged shout for help.

"Hope they come," and "Bet they'll come," the Hubert Laneites were saying hopefully. They'd enjoyed yesterday's fight and wanted another. Suddenly Queenie, panting and breathless, arrived on the scene.

She exchanged a quick wink with Hubert before she began:

"William's sent me. He says it's off. The Red Heads aren't coming. They've all gone to a cricket match in Hadley. An' he says Farmer Smith's having a rat hunt in his barn an' he's going there, so you'd better go too."

The Hubert Laneites set off at an eager run towards Farmer Smith's barn.

Only Queenie and Hubert remained. They exchanged another wink. Hubert couldn't wink properly but he did his best.

"They're comin'," whispered Queenie. "Let's go nearer an' watch them."

They went nearer and watched them. It was—to them—a glorious sight. The Red Heads arrived in full force and fell upon the unsuspecting Outlaws. William's cry for help rang out again and again—always without avail, for the Hubert Laneites were beyond earshot, hastening gleefully to Farmer Smith's barn. The Outlaws fought bravely, but their bravery only earned them the more punishment, and in the end they turned ingloriously to flight. But the Red Heads wanted more than victory. Yesterday one of their band had been taken prisoner. To wipe out the disgrace, they must take one of the Outlaws prisoner—if possible their leader. It was quite easy, for William was the last to turn to flee, and was quickly secured. The rest of his band was too intent on flight to see what happened. Only Ginger, looking back at the bend of the road, saw the capture and turned to follow furtively in the shelter of the hedge.

The headquarters of the Red Heads was an empty house called Fairmead just outside the village. It had stood empty for many years and was likely to stand empty for many more. Every window was broken. The paint was peeling off the woodwork. The roof let the rain into most of the rooms, while dry and every other kind of rot infested the whole place. It was owned by an old man called Daniel Smith, who had a flat bald head, Jewish nose, cross eyes, and a wispy grey beard. He lived in another derelict but smaller house nearby and looked almost as tumbledown as his property. He earned his living (apparently) by renting a few bad meadows, a few worse cottages, keeping poultry and buying and selling everything from house property to old iron. He was known to the Outlaws as Cross-eye Smith and had always been a virulent enemy of theirs. His son, Rube, helped his father in the business and shared fully his dislike of boys in general and the Outlaws in particular, chasing them away with stones and bricks whenever they approached his property.

It was a mystery why they allowed the Red Heads to occupy Fairmead without reprisals, but so far they seemed to have made no effort to turn them out.

To this spot, then, William was dragged by his captors, thrust into the only room that boasted a key, and locked in. So fierce had been the conflict, so breathless the capture, that for a minute or two he hardly realised what had happened. Then he sat up and examined his injuries. He was bruised all over, one eye was slowly closing and there was a lump on his forehead the size of an egg, but otherwise he seemed to be unharmed. He climbed to his feet and inspected his prison. The door was locked. He examined the window. The catch had rusted together so as to be immovable, and, though the panes were broken, there was no one hole large enough to afford egress to his body without increasing his already considerable injuries. After a short inspection he gave up hope of escape by that means and returned to the door. A murmur of voices told him that the Red Heads were holding a conference outside. To his surprise he heard Queenie's voice among them. The Red Heads were describing to her the success of her scheme. Too late he realised what had happened. His only comfort was that he had been justified in his distrust of girls. . . .

"I thought of it, didn't I?" she was saying aggressively. "You wouldn't have had any chance at all if it hadn't been for me."

"All right," said the strident voice of Red Head. "We've made you a member of the gang, haven't we?"

"Well, I oughter be a jolly high-up member," Queenie was saying. "It was all my plan. If it hadn't been for me bein' so clever you'd never 've got *near* 'em. That rotten ole William Brown! Coo, I'm glad you took *him* prisoner." She approached her mouth to the keyhole of the room where William was and began to jeer at him. "Who's been took prisoner? *Yah!* Who thought he was everybody an' got took prisoner? *Yah!* Who got licked? Who said girls were no good? *Yah!* P'raps you wish you'd let a girl help *you* now, don't you? *Yah!*"

By exercise of great self-control William managed to preserve a masterly silence, and Queenie gradually tired of the process of taunting him. The Red Heads tired of it much more quickly.

"Aw, come on!" said Red Head. "I'm not goin' to waste all afternoon here."

"What about the prisoner?" said someone,

"We'll let him go," said Red Head.

"Let him *go*?" shrilled Queenie. "After all the trouble I've had gettin' him took prisoner? An' now you jus' say 'Let him go'! I wouldn't've done it if I'd known that."

"Well, we can't keep him here all night," said Red Head. "We'd have the cops after us."

"No, but you can keep him here till bedtime," said

"WHO'S BEEN TOOK PRISONER? *YAH!*" SAID QUEENIE
THROUGH THE KEYHOLE OF THE ROOM IN WHICH WILLIAM
WAS SHUT.

Queenie. "He's *my* enemy an' I'm not *goin'* to have him
let go."

"Aw, all right," said Red Head. "Have your own
way. We'll leave him here till bedtime, then. Come
on. . . ."

Their voices died away in the distance, Queenie
continuing to shout taunts monotonously till she was out
of hearing.

Almost at once there came the sound of the turning of

the key in the lock, and Ginger entered.

"I had to wait till they'd gone," he explained. "I say, that awful girl was with them."

"Don't I *know*!" groaned William. "It was her all the time. If it hadn't been for her we'd never have got licked. She's a rotten ole crook, that's what she is, an' so is that rotten ole Hubert. . . . Well, let's get out of it now."

But Ginger, who had gone across to the window, drew back hastily and spoke in a horror-struck whisper.

"There's ole Cross-eye Smith an' Rube comin' here. They'll *murder* us if they find us. Let's hide, quick."

The only possible hiding place was a wooden cupboard built in the wall, and into this William and Ginger with some difficulty accommodated themselves. The door would not quite close on them, but William, crouching on the top of Ginger, held it as nearly closed as possible. They heard Cross-eye and Rube come into the house and go round it, looking into every room. When they looked into the room where William and Ginger were, William in his excitement grabbed Ginger's hair so tightly that Ginger gave a gasp, but Cross-eye and Rube did not hear. They went out, leaving the door open, and continued their inspection of the other rooms, talking in thick strident voices that were plainly audible to the two boys.

"See! It's what I told you," said Cross-eye. "Used by boys. Littered up with their stuff and *fires* made. Fires made every day by the look of it."

It struck William as strange that Cross-eye should not sound at all annoyed by this discovery. He sounded, on the contrary, excited and exultant.

"Straw and sacking everywhere," he went on. "Some of them must have been sleeping here. That young fool in charge of them wouldn't know whether they were in the camp or not. And all the wood's as dry as tinder. The windows are all broke, too. That'll make a good draught. The place is insured for £2,000, and I couldn't get it off my hands if I tried to *give* it away."

"The fire engine may get here too quick," suggested Rube.

"Not it! Has to come from Hadley. An' there's no water. Pump cemented in. Why, man, it won't be *seen* till it's too late to do anything. It'll be blamed on those boys with their fires and rubbish. Look! Cigarette ends, too. It's a dead cert."

William and Ginger, beyond being mildly surprised at Cross-eye's inexplicable lack of indignation with the trespassers on his property, took no interest in this conversation. Their ears were strained anxiously for sounds of departure. At last they came. The front door was shut with a bang and the strident voices died away in the distance. Tumbling out of the cupboard, and crouching beneath the window, William and Ginger watched the two men walk away, still talking and gesticulating.

"Gosh!" gasped Ginger. "You nearly squashed my head in sittin' on the top of me like that."

"Well, you nearly gave the show away, lettin' out a yell like what you did."

"Well, you were pullin' out my hair by the roots."

"*Roots!*" jeered William. "Your hair's not got no roots. You've no brains for it to take root in. Come on. Let's get out now. Crumbs! I'm all stiff, aren't you?"

Looking cautiously around them, they went out of the front door and hurried home.

"I'd get even with that ole Queenie," said William, "if it wasn't a waste of time gettin' even with a rotten ole girl."

"We'll have to do *somethin'*," said Ginger.

"Well, we'll think of it to-morrow," said William. "I've had enough for one day."

*   *   *

But the next day all other sensations were dwarfed by the news of the fire at Fairmead. It had raged during the night, and the fire engine from Hadley had arrived too late to do much even if there had been any adequate water supply, which there was not. The place was practically burnt out.

William heard his family discussing the matter at lunch.

"It was all caused by those dreadful boys from the camp," said Mrs. Brown. "They'd been making fires there, and some of them even sleeping there. The insurance agent came down this morning, and they found traces of them all over the place."

"Smith's quite capable of planting traces of anything anywhere," put in Robert.

William was not listening to the conversation. He was rehearsing to himself various cutting phrases which he hoped to bring out with telling effect when he met Queenie. ("Cheats never prosper." "Who's a dirty dog?" "Jus' like a rotten ole girl!" . . .)

"Oh, but he didn't," said Mrs. Brown.

"How do you know?" said Robert.

("Cheats never prosper." "Jus' like a rotten ole girl.")

"What are you muttering about, William?" said Mrs. Brown.

"Nothin'," said William, attacking his helping of suet pudding as savagely as if it were the Queenie it somewhat resembled.

"Well, the agent went to the camp and interviewed these boys," said Mrs. Brown to Robert, "and they admitted having used the house and made fires there and taken straw and sacking there to sleep on. And they'd smoked cigarettes there, though smoking's against the rules of the camp. They've got into very serious trouble about it, of course. It's the worst managed camp we've ever had in the village. It's a good thing it's breaking up to-morrow."

"Jus' like a rotten cheatin' ole girl," muttered William, shovelling the last spoonful of pudding into his mouth ferociously. "Can I go, please?"

"He seems upset about something," said Mrs. Brown, watching William's retreating figure with vague concern.

"Oh no, he isn't," Robert reassured her. "He's only mad. Mad as a hatter. Always has been. . . . Lucky for old Smith, isn't it, though, that fire!"

William and Ginger had decided to go to Hubert's house, face him with his treachery, and insist on satisfaction. They had not, however, to go as far as that, for they came upon Hubert and Queenie walking down the road near the station. William let loose his carefully prepared stream of insults, but the enemy at once started a counter-offensive of equal intensity.

"Cheats never prosper."

"Who got took prisoner? Yah!"

"Who's a dirty dog?"

"Who got locked up?"

"Jus' like a rotten ole girl."

"Who said girls weren't any good an' then wished he hadn't?"

"I *didn't* wish I hadn't. They're rotten ole cheats."

"Who got took prisoner?"

"Cheats never prosper."

A young man coming down the road towards the station lingered to listen with idle amusement to this

interchange of personalities. He was the representative
of the insurance society that had just agreed to pay Mr.
Smith the £2,000 for his burnt house. He had had a tiring
morning, interviewing the Smiths and the boys from the
camp, and he wanted to get back home. But the local
train service was not accommodating, and he had had
over an hour to wait for his train. So he loitered about,
deriving what entertainment he could from the limited
resources of the place. He had watched a hen scratching
the surface of the road for about ten minutes and was
tiring of the spectacle. This first-class juvenile row,
springing up suddenly on the highway under his nose,
was a welcome diversion. The interchanges were
spirited if a trifle monotonous.

"Rotten ole cheats, that's what you are."

"Who got took prisoner an' locked up?"

"Mean ole cheats. Wish it'd been a *real* war.
You'd've got shot, an' jolly well serve you right."

"Wish you'd still been in that ole house when it caught
fire. You'd've got burnt up an' jolly well serve *you*
right."

The young man pricked up his ears. His air of list-
less boredom fell from him. He became alert and
businesslike.

"I say," he said to William, interrupting the row
unceremoniously, "did they shut you up in that house
that was burnt yesterday?"

"Huh!" said William with a short laugh. "That's
nothin' to me. Minute they'd gone one of my men came
an' let me out. At least it *would*'ve been the minute
they'd gone if that old Cross-eye Smith an' Rube hadn't
come an' we had to wait till they'd gone 'fore we
escaped."

The young man became still more alert and
businesslike.

"Cross-eye Smith? Do you mean Smith, the owner of the house?"

"Yes," agreed William, "that ole cross-eyed cross-patch."

"Are you *sure*?" said the young man. "He said he'd not been near the place for over a week."

"'Course I'm sure," said William impatiently. "Didn't me an' Ginger *see* 'em come in and didn't we wait an' listen to 'em talkin' a lot of nonsense about fires an' what-not before we could get out?"

The young man was no longer merely alert and businesslike. He was definitely excited. He took out a little note-book.

"Can you remember exactly what you heard them say?" he said.

"'Course I can," said William proudly. "I've got a jolly good memory. So's Ginger. I c'n tell you jolly well *everythin'* they said. An' so can Ginger."

A few minutes later the young man closed the note-book. His face wore a look of seraphic content.

Hubert and Queenie were watching, open-mouthed with bewilderment.

The young man glanced at his watch. His train was nearly due. He was turning away when a sudden thought struck him and he turned back.

"By the way," he said, "what would you two boys like best?"

William gaped at him for a moment, then collected his forces and said:

"A bicycle."

"Well," said the young man, "I think I can promise that to both of you. It looks as if you've saved my company £2,000. If you have, I don't think they'll strain at a couple of bicycles."

Queenie suddenly found her voice. "D'you mean

you're goin' to give *him* a bicycle?" she said shrilly, pointing to William.

"Of course," said the young man simply.

"An' not to *me*?"

The young man smiled. Though his acquaintance with Queenie was a short one, he did not find her an attractive child.

"I see no reason at all why we should give you one," he said. "In any case I gather that you didn't come too well out of the affair. . . . Well, I must go now. Oh," to William and Ginger, "just give me your names and addresses. The bicycles should be along some time next week."

Still in a sort of trance, William and Ginger gave their names and addresses. The young man put his note-book in his pocket, took his leave of them, and set off down the road towards the station.

The four children stood and looked at each other in silence for a few moments. Then William said in a faint whisper:

"Gosh! A bicycle!"

Queenie's face had gone from pink to red, from red to purple, then suddenly she burst into sobs of rage and turned on Hubert.

"It's all your fault, you hateful boy!" she said. "It's all your fault!"

She flung herself upon him, pulling at his hair with both hands. He yelled and turned to flee. She pursued him down the road. Their howls rent the air of the peaceful countryside.

William and Ginger neither saw nor heard. They stood there staring at each other. Finally William said again:

"*Gosh!* A bicycle."

THE END